STAR TURN

Afterwards, in the changing room, Jessamy said, 'You *are* a dancer, aren't you?'

Karen hesitated; then nodded rather bashfully as she pulled her T-shirt over her head.

'I knew you were!' Jessamy was triumphant. 'I said as soon as I saw you, that's a dancer if ever there was.' She turned and did a ballet dancer's walk the length of the cloakroom and back, toes pointed, arms in first. 'I can spot a dancer a hundred metres off.'

Susan chimed in: 'Her mother – ' she pointed dramatically at Jessamy ' – was Belinda Tarrant!'

She still was, of course, only her dancing days were long since over. Now she ran the Tarrant Academy of Dance.

Star Turn

Jean Ure

RED FOX

A Red Fox Book

Published by Random House Children's Books
20 Vauxhall Bridge Road, London SW1V 2SA

A division of Random House UK Ltd
London Melbourne Sydney Auckland
Johannesburg and agencies throughout the world

Copyright © Jean Ure 1993

1 3 5 7 9 10 8 6 4 2

First published by Hutchinson Children's Books 1993

Red Fox edition 1994

Printed and bound in Great Britain by
Cox & Wyman Ltd, Reading, Berkshire

RANDOM HOUSE UK Limited Reg. No. 954009

ISBN 0 09 925091 8

1

There were five new girls in Year 7 at the start of the winter term at Coombe Hurst School. Jessamy studied them, critically.

Four of them were quite ordinary – no different from all the other Year 7s in their brown-and-orange uniforms. Lumpy, Gangly, Clever and Beach Ball, thought Jessamy, rapidly nicknaming them to herself.

Lumpy was rather plain and dim looking; Gangly was tall, and beanstalk thin; Clever wore glasses and a worried frown; Beach Ball was pretty, but rounded and plump as a blown-up balloon.

Jessamy dismissed them; they held no interest for her. The one who caught her eye, as they filed self-consciously into morning assembly and tacked on to the end of the Year 7 line, was the one at the back.

'There's a dancer if ever I saw one!' thought Jessamy. She tended sometimes to think rather mature thoughts for an eleven-year-old; it came from being the youngest in the family, with a brother and sister who were both grown-up.

Jessamy had only a quick glimpse of the girl-who-was-a-dancer because Jessamy was at one end of the line and the dancer at the other, and Miss Shergold, the Head Mistress, would go all icy and sarcastic if she noticed Jessamy leaning forward and peering.

In spite of Miss Shergold, she saw enough to convince her: the girl *had* to be a dancer. She was tiny and trim and beautifully proportioned – a small, well-shaped head on a slender neck, which was exactly what you needed for ballet (no good being a pumpkin head and hoping to dance Giselle), with narrow hips and lovely long legs which Jessamy immediately envied.

Jessamy had good legs, but hers were made for beats and jumps rather than for the perfect *arabesque*. Jessamy had already, rather sadly, faced up to the fact that she probably wasn't ever going to dance Giselle. It wasn't only her legs. She had heard her mum and dad discussing it one day. Her dad had said, 'She has too robust a personality.' Her mum had agreed: Jessamy was more of a Swanhilda than a Giselle.

Jessamy didn't actually mind being a Swanhilda – *Coppélia* was one of her favourite ballets – though the part she really wanted to dance was the Miller's Wife in Massine's *Three-Cornered Hat*. That was something the new girl would never be offered, with her flaxen hair.

It was a pity about the hair. Blonde hair was lovely, of course, and one or two great dancers had been fair – Pamela May, for example, who had been with the Sadler's Wells Ballet long before Jessamy was even born – but black was best. It showed up better on stage. On the other hand, blonde was perfect for the Queen of the Wilis.

Jessamy whiled away the time during the usual beginning-of-term announcements ('No food to be eaten in the classrooms. Brown shoes with white socks or brown tights to be worn *at all times*') by mentally staging her own private production of *Giselle* with the new girl as Myrthe and herself, improbably, as Giselle. She was just deciding who she would have for her Albrecht – Erik Bruhn? Rudolf Nureyev? Her own brother? *Nijinsky*? – when the music started up for the end of assembly and Year 7, with the new girl now in the lead, filed out being Mrs Truelove, their form mistress.

By craning forward just a little, Jessamy could see that the new girl already walked like a dancer, even though she was only eleven. She had either been having ballet lessons for years or she was blessed with good natural turnout. Jessamy wasn't jealous because Jessamy had good natural turnout, as well.

'Do you mind?' hissed a Year 8, pushing at her.

Jessamy slipped back into the ranks and followed meekly behind the others – well, as meekly as she ever could. Jessamy wasn't really a meek sort of person. 'Assertive' was how she had been described on her report last summer.

Mrs Truelove had already assigned the new girls to places at the front of the room, where she could keep an eye on them. Jessamy, as soon as she had arrived at school, had bagged three desks right at the back for herself and her two best friends, Sheela Shah and Susan Garibaldi. She couldn't see the new girl from where she sat, but when Mrs Truelove took the register she started with the name 'Karen Anders', which was definitely new. A small but clear voice said, 'Yes, miss.'

Mrs Truelove looked up from the register.

'I do have a name, Karen . . . it's Mrs Truelove. Shall we start again?'

Sheela and Susan grinned, but Jessamy felt sorry for

9

the new girl, being shown up like that. They had always heard, in Juniors, that Mrs Truelove could be mean. Not that Jessamy cared two straws: teachers could be as mean as they liked and it just rolled right off Jessamy. It was rotten to be mean to a new girl, though. She could only hope that the new girl, like Jessamy herself, didn't care a fig for anything except dancing; that way, it really didn't matter if people had a go at you or accused you of being stupid at ordinary lessons. Jessamy was stupid at everything except English, art, music and French, and it didn't bother her in the slightest. Why should a ballet dancer need to be able to use computers and do mental arithmetic?

With all the business of electing monitors and filling in timetables, Jessamy didn't think about the new girl again until breaktime, when she looked round the playground and saw her standing with one of the other new ones, the one who looked serious and clever. The serious one was talking, very earnestly; the dancer was listening politely, trying to pretend an interest. Jessamy could tell that she was pretending. She was standing with her arms in a low fifth, her hands loosely clasped, and her feet in third, and Jessamy just knew that she was itching to look down and check her position, check her ankles weren't rolling in (they weren't: she had a *very* good turnout). Her blonde hair was tied back in a pony tail. Jessamy had worn hers in plaits when they were in Juniors, but now she was in Senior School she wore it loose, with a hair band. Probably, one day quite soon, Mrs Truelove would tell her to 'Do something about your hair, please, Jessamy.' They didn't like you having it all round your shoulders. Jessamy thought it made a nice change from having to scrape it back the way you did for ballet class.

'Hey!' Susan jiggled at her elbow. 'What are you goggling at?'

'Not goggling at anything,' said Jessamy, but she couldn't help a small backwards glance as she walked away, arm in arm with Susan and Sheela.

Jessamy had been best friends with Susan and Sheela all the way up through Juniors; they did everything together and almost never quarrelled. Jessamy certainly wasn't thinking of *not* being friends with them any more, but the small wistful thought occurred to her that it would be fun to have an ally – someone who shared her own passion for the ballet. Someone who knew what *entrechats* were and didn't go all silly and giggly when she talked of *ports de bras*.

'*Bra*?'

'Did you say *bra*?'

Ooh! Naughty! Squeak squeak giggle giggle.

Jessamy sighed. They couldn't help it; you had to be patient. The only trouble was, Jessamy wasn't at all a patient sort of person.

'Let's go and sit on a bench,' said Sheela. 'I've got something to show you.'

Sheela had brought in a teen magazine which she had borrowed from the shelves of her dad's newsagent's. What she and Susan liked to do was turn to the problem page, which was always full of gigglesome (but highly spicy) questions about love and sex and *bodies*.

Sheela said, 'It isn't porn. It's learning about things.'

'It's being prepared,' said Susan.

Jessamy was quite interested in the love and sex, but didn't share Sheela and Susan's fascination with bodies – well, she *was* fascinated by bodies, her own principally, but not in any gigglesome sense. Jessamy was fascinated by the way her body worked and what she was able to do with it. She thought she probably saw it rather like a violinist saw his violin: as an instrument. For Susan and Sheela, bodies were exciting and giggly. Jessamy sometimes felt superior and sometimes felt that maybe she was missing out.

'Listen to *this*,' said Sheela, in tones of shocked delight. 'My boyfriend – '

The new girl was coming across the playground with the serious one. The serious one (Jessamy thought her name might be Portia Wetherall, except how could you call anyone *Portia*?) shambled, with slouched shoulders. The dancer – she knew her name was Karen Anders, but she didn't quite feel ready to think of her as Karen; she was still too new for that – walked as if she were being pulled by an invisible string from the crown of her head. Good, thought Jessamy. She nodded approvingly, and smiled. The new girl, as if not quite sure the smile was intended for her, smiled back uncertainly.

Susan and Sheela, meanwhile, were sitting with heads bent over their teen mag. Jessamy could see that Susan's face was bright crimson. Sheela's almost certainly would have been had her skin not been too dark for it to show. They had obviously found something that excited them.

'Wow!' breathed Susan.

'Do you think that is *true*?' said Sheela.

'Must be, if it's in a magazine.'

'In that case,' said Sheela, 'I am not ever, *ever*, going to get married.'

'Safer to be a nun,' said Susan.

'Oh, but I can't be!' Sheela's wails rent the playground. 'I'm not a Christian!'

'You'll have to convert.'

'My dad won't let me! He'll make me get married! God, it's horrible,' moaned Sheela, enjoying herself.

They did this sort of thing, sometimes: frightened themselves silly. Secretly they loved it.

After break they had maths with Mrs Allan, when Jessamy was predictably slow to grasp the principle of subtracting decimal fractions, and the new girl not very much better. If you gave Jessamy a complicated *enchaînement*, or series of steps, to perform she could pick them up immediately, no problem. Figures confused her. The serious girl, whose name *was* Portia, turned out to be some kind of mathematical genius, which confused Mrs Allan: they weren't used to geniuses at Coombe Hurst.

The last period before lunch was gym. For years and years, Jessamy had been the star gymnast of her group. Miss Mayle, in Juniors, had wanted her to train seriously, but of course she couldn't do that. Jessamy's mother wouldn't hear of it. Sometimes she even grew twitchy at the thought of Jessamy just jumping over boxes or shinning up ropes.

'Your arms, Jessamy! Your arms! You'll end up looking like a coal heaver!'

Some day soon she would probably put her foot down, but she hadn't as yet, which meant that Jessamy was still free to bounce about and show off. The new girl didn't show off, and she didn't bounce, either, but she certainly challenged Jessamy's position as star gymnast. She was every bit as supple, every bit as neat, had just as good balance and landed just as lightly. Jessamy didn't mind. It only went to confirm her diagnosis: another dancer had come to Coombe Hurst.

At the end of the period Miss Northgate said, 'Well! Congratulations to Jessamy – and congratulations to Karen, too! I look forward to working with you two girls. I hope you all noticed how gracefully they did everything? How light they are on their feet? I'd expect it from Jessamy, of course – but it seems we have another little gymnast in our midst!'

Karen's cheeks grew slightly pink, as everyone turned to look first at her and then rather slyly at Jessamy, to see how she was taking it. Jessamy took it perfectly calmly. She had no ambitions as a gymnast, and anyway Karen's style was quite different from hers. Karen was obviously going to be one of those dancers who were blessed with line: Jessamy had elevation. They weren't in competition.

Afterwards, in the changing room, Jessamy said, 'You *are* a dancer, aren't you?'

Karen hesitated; then nodded rather bashfully as she pulled her T-shirt over her head.

'I knew you were!' Jessamy was triumphant. 'I said as soon as I saw you, that's a dancer if ever there was.' She turned and did a ballet dancer's walk the length of the cloakroom and back, toes pointed, arms in first. 'I can spot a dancer a hundred metres off!'

Susan chimed in: 'Her mother – ' she pointed dramatically at Jessamy ' – was Belinda Tarrant!'

She still was, of course, only her dancing days were long since over. Now she ran the Tarrant Academy of Dance.

'Yes, and her dad is Ben Hart,' said Sheela, who hadn't the faintest idea, when it came to it, what Jessamy's dad actually did, except that it was something to do with ballet. (In fact he flew about the world putting on productions for people.) 'And her *brother* – ' Sheela paused, importantly ' – her brother is Saul Hart of the City Ballet Company.'

Karen's face, by now, was bright pillar-box red. She turned to Jessamy with eyes huge as satellite dishes (her eyes were bright blue: they would photograph beautifully, thought Jessamy). Karen obviously knew all about Ben and Saul Hart, and Belinda Tarrant, which was more than Susan and Sheela would have done if Jessamy hadn't told them.

'It's true!' said Susan.

Karen nodded, shyly. 'I can see it now.'

'She looks just like him,' said Sheela.

Jessamy did bear quite a strong resemblance to Saul – and to her dad. Both Saul and her dad were short and dark and compact. Belinda Tarrant, on the other hand, was long-limbed and red-haired (red-haired with a bit of help these days, as she ruefully admitted). Jacquetta took after her – the same glorious legs that went on for ever, the same burnished hair – only Jack had let the family down by throwing away her ballet shoes for a life of domestic bliss.

'Jessamy's going to be a ballerina,' said Susan.

15

'Prima donna ballerina,' said Sheela.

Jessamy did wish they wouldn't. She knew they were proud of her and liked to display her to people, but it wasn't in good taste to boast about her like that – especially when they got the terminology all wrong. Prima donna ballerina!

Jessamy tried to catch Karen's eye, but Karen, seemingly overwhelmed to think that she was at school with the daughter of Ben Hart and Belinda Tarrant, was struggling, scarlet-faced, into her skirt. Bother! Now she probably wouldn't dare to talk to Jessamy. She would think Jessamy was going to be too grand. There were some people – pushy people – who would instantly tap into her like leeches, but she could see already that Karen wasn't one of those. That at least was a relief. Ballet classes were full of them. *And* their mothers.

'Where do you learn?' said Jessamy, manoeuvring herself so that she was between Karen and the others. 'Somewhere local?'

'Mm.' Karen nodded, and ducked her head as she pulled on her sweater.

'In Chiswick?'

'Mm.'

'At a school? Or privately?'

There was a pause.

'Privately,' said Karen.

'What, individual lessons?' Karen's parents must be rich as rich! Even Jessamy, whose mother owned her own school, didn't very often have individual lessons. 'Who with?'

'I don't think you'd have heard of her,' said Karen,

16

taking the elastic band off her ponytail, shaking her hair out and putting it back in the elastic band.

'I bet I would!' Jessamy knew all the dancing schools and all the teachers in the whole of Chiswick; practically the whole of London. 'Try me! What's her name?'

'I just call her Madame . . . Madame Olga.'

'Is she Russian?'

'Yes. She used to dance with Diaghilev.'

Heavens! She must be positively ancient.

'What's her surname?' said Jessamy.

'I can't remember. I can never pronounce it. Something like . . . Spess – '

'Spessivtseva? Olga Spessivtseva?'

'No, not her,' said Karen.

Jessamy relaxed. Olga Spessivtseva was famous. (Though come to think of it she probably wasn't still alive. She made a note to ask her mum.)

'Is she old?' said Jessamy.

'Quite,' said Karen.

'I'll see if my mum knows her. She knows everybody.'

They left the gym together, with Susan and Sheela close behind and Portia hovering.

'How many lessons do you have a week?' said Jessamy.

'Every afternoon after school and Saturday mornings.' Karen said it proudly, almost defiantly. Jessamy widened her eyes: she only had four lessons a week, and then not private.

'What syllabus are you doing?'

'Oh . . . just what Madame chooses.'

'So are you going to take it up professionally?'

Karen's face grew crimson again.

'I'd like to.' She looked enviously at Jessamy. 'I suppose you are?'

'Got to, haven't I?' said Jessamy.

Karen's blue eyes widened again, this time in shocked disbelief.

'Don't you want to?'

'Oh, yes,' said Jessamy. 'It's just that even if I didn't, it wouldn't make any difference. They're relying on me, you see, 'cause of Jack going and letting them down. She's my sister. She's only twenty-one and having *babies* already.'

Susan and Sheela groaned in unison.

'She won't ever go back to ballet,' said Jessamy. 'She says she's had enough of it. Mum was furious. She said she might at least have waited, like Mum did. Mum didn't start having babies till she was past her prime. That's what she always says ... "*I didn't even think about you lot till I was past my prime.*" She didn't think about me at all,' said Jessamy. 'I was a mistake.'

'A night of mad passionate love,' said Sheela.

Portia looked at her rather wildly. Susan giggled.

'Take no notice,' said Jessamy. 'They've just discovered sex.'

Portia's eyes came out on stalks.

'They talk about sex all the time,' said Jessamy. 'They're obsessed by it.' She turned cosily to Karen. 'I must say, it'll be nice to have someone else here who's a dancer. There's a girl in Year 9 who does tap, and some of the kids do jazz dancing, but until you came I was the only one who did ballet. It'll be nice to have someone I can talk to and know they'll understand what I'm talking about. These two – ' she jerked her thumb at the still sniggering Susan and Sheela ' – they are just so dead ignorant it's unbelievable. They think *posé* means a bunch of flowers!'

Karen giggled, and then clapped a hand to her mouth as if she shouldn't have done.

'Oh, you don't have to worry about them,' said Jessamy. 'They know they're ignorant – I'm always telling them.'

'So what is a posy?' said Sheela.

Instantly, as one, Karen and Jessamy took up their positions, lifted a leg and stepped forward onto it.

'That's a posy?' said Sheela.

'Doesn't look like very much to me,' said Susan.

'It isn't very much. It isn't meant to be very much.'

'It just means to take a step, really,' explained Karen.

Susan and Sheela looked at each other. Susan tapped a finger to her forehead.

'It's French,' said Portia, coming unexpectedly to life.

'Ballet terms always are,' said Jessamy. 'I'll ask my mum when I get home if she knows your Madame Olga.'

'She won't,' said Karen.

'I bet she will,' said Jessamy. 'She knows everyone.'

2

'Mum,' said Jessamy, 'do you know a ballet teacher called Madame Olga?'

'Never heard of her.' Belinda Tarrant was checking the proofs of the new prospectus for the Tarrant Academy of Ballet. 'Look at that!' Crossly, she snatched up her red pen and made angry squiggles on the page. 'I sometimes think printers are halfwits.'

'She used to dance with Diaghilev,' said Jessamy.

'Who did?'

'Madame Olga.'

'Rubbish!' said her mum, making more marks.

'She did,' insisted Jessamy. 'Karen said so.'

Belinda Tarrant raised her head at last. She looked at Jessamy over the tops of her spectacles.

'And who may Karen happen to be?'

'Karen Anders.'

'And who is Karen Anders?'

'She's a girl at school. She just started, today.'

'And what does she know about anything?'

Losing interest, Belinda Tarrant went back to her proofs. It was sometimes very difficult holding any normal sort of conversation with her; she was always so busy. If she wasn't teaching, she was travelling up to town to meet people, or on the phone to Dad in Canada or Japan or wherever he happened to be, or auditioning new pupils for the Academy, or giving interviews for radio and television. Jessamy supposed that was what came of having a mother who wasn't quite ordinary.

'Karen knows about her because she has lessons from her. She can't pronounce her surname properly. She thinks it begins "Spess" something.'

'If she's trying to tell you she's Olga Spessivtseva you can forget it. She must have died years ago and even if she hadn't she'd be far too old to teach.'

'She is old. But anyway it wasn't Olga Spessivtseva, just someone who sounds like her.'

'Honestly!' Her mum pounced again, with her red pen. 'Drivel!' she cried. 'Total and utter drivel!'

Jessamy knew when she was beaten. If Dad had been here she could have asked him, though he didn't know all the local teachers as well as Mum did, but Dad was in New York staging a revival of Frederick Ashton's *Symphonic Variations* for ABT. (When she had mentioned it to Susan and Sheela they had thought she was talking about a television station. They had actually never heard of American Ballet Theater!)

Karen would be good in *Symphonic Variations*, she thought, reluctantly trailing upstairs to make a start on some homework. It was an abstract ballet, without any storyline. It was one of Belinda Tarrant's favourites (she had danced in it at Covent Garden with Margot Fonteyn) though Jessamy preferred romantic ballets where you could do a bit of acting and give your emotions full reign.

Jessamy sometimes thought that if anything awful ever happened to stop her doing ballet – just suppose, horror of horrors, that she grew too big or the wrong shape – she wouldn't mind taking up acting. She always felt slightly wistful, when the school end-of-term productions were planned, at being passed over as a possible actress. It was always, 'Well, Jessamy! May we expect the usual contribution from you?' The usual contribution was a solo dance, made up by Jessamy herself, to fit in with the theme of whatever play they were doing. Maybe this term she and Karen could do it together? Or better still – she plumped herself down at her desk – maybe Karen could do it and Jessamy could act?

The trouble was, people were such snobs. Just because Jessamy came from a famous family and Karen didn't, or at least not as far as she knew, they were bound to insist that Jessamy danced the same as usual, so that they could write about her in the programme: 'Jessamy Hart comes from a famous family of dancers. Her mother, Belinda Tarrant', etc., etc.

Same old thing, every year. You'd have thought people would be sick of it by now.

Moodily, Jessamy unscrewed the top of her fountain pen and pulled a block of squared paper towards her. Mrs Allan had actually gone and set them some homework. On their first day back! She would complain to her mum if they got too much. Belinda Tarrant had chosen Coombe Hurst specially because it had a reputation for not pushing people too hard. Since Jessamy was going to be a dancer, ballet had to have first priority, particularly above beastly maths.

Fifteen minutes later, Jessamy had scamped through her decimal fractions, stuffed everything back into her school bag and was stretched out on her bed reading the autobiography of Gelsey Kirkland, whom Saul and Jacquetta had once been lucky enough to see dancing Juliet with the Royal Ballet. Jessamy had been too young, just as she had been for so many things. But that was why it was important to read about all the great dancers whom she had never been able to see. Far more useful than messing about with decimals and fractions and idiotic jumping dots (especially as she could never decide which way they were supposed to jump).

'I asked my mum about your Madame Olga,' said Jessamy, as she and Karen met up next day on their way to school. 'You were quite right. She hasn't heard of her.'

'She's very old,' said Karen. 'Practically retired. She only takes one or two pupils.'

'Did you have to audition for her?'

'Yes – well. Sort of. I hadn't started learning then.'

'But she could tell.' Jessamy nodded. 'My mum always says that she can tell almost just by looking at someone. She says you get a feel for it. I bet you were thrilled when she accepted you?'

'Yes,' said Karen, but she didn't actually sound very thrilled. Jessamy regarded her, doubtfully. Maybe Madame Olga wasn't quite as good as she sounded. Too old, perhaps.

'If ever you want to change teachers,' she said, 'you could always come to my mum's school.'

'Do they do scholarships?' Karen asked it eagerly, her blue eyes alight and sparkling.

'Not scholarships exactly, but sometimes if people

are deserving and can't afford the fees, Mum will only charge half price.'

The sparkle went out of Karen's eyes. Surely her parents couldn't be short of money? Not sending her to Coombe Hurst. Coombe Hurst might not be very academic, but it cost the earth, at least according to Jessamy's mum. Daylight robbery, she called it.

'I expect I shall stay with Madame Olga for a while,' said Karen. 'I've got used to the way she teaches.'

'Well, that is important,' agreed Jessamy, 'so long as she's good. *Is* she good?'

'I – I think so,' said Karen.

'Perhaps I should come and watch a class?' Karen looked startled. 'Then I could tell you,' said Jessamy. She didn't mean to sound boastful, but she had had enough experience to know a good teacher when she saw one.

Karen shook her head.

'Madame Olga doesn't allow anyone in,' she said.

Karen's special friend at Coombe Hurst was obviously going to be the serious-minded Portia, but nonetheless circumstances threw her and Jessamy together quite often. In movement class, Miss Shaw singled out Karen and Jessamy to demonstrate.

'Let's see what you two girls can do,' she said. They had been improvising to some beautiful music called Albinoni's Adagio, very slow and dreamy. 'Everyone sit down and watch Karen and Jessamy. I shall expect some real dancing from you two,' she added.

Jessamy was too busy with her own improvisation to see what Karen was doing, but it was obviously good for as the music came to an end there was a silence, followed by a burst of applause.

'Thank you,' said Miss Shaw. 'Thank you, both of you. That showed real feeling for the music.'

Quite often, because by now everyone knew that Karen was a dancer as well as Jessamy, people would come up to them and say, 'Can you do the splits?' 'Can you bend over backwards?' 'Can you lift your leg up behind you and touch the back of your head?'

'It's not really ballet,' Jessamy would say, 'it's just showing off.'

'So go on, then! Show off!'

Jessamy never minded obliging. Karen was shyer, but usually did it in the end.

'It's just acrobatics,' Jessamy would explain.

'And what,' demanded a big, fierce Year 8 on one occasion, 'is wrong with acrobatics?'

'N–nothing,' stammered Karen.

'In the right place,' added Jessamy.

'Don't you do those things when you have classes?' said Portia.

'Sometimes. Not always. Not like *pliés* and *ronds de jambes* and – '

The Year 8 exploded.

'There they go! Spouting Frog! Why can't you just say knees bends?'

''Cause they're not,' said Jessamy.

The Year 8 made a rude noise. Jessamy had discovered that there were some people – not just Year 8s, but grown-up people, as well – who looked down their noses at the thought of anyone learning ballet. Her mum, only the other day, had exploded in rage at an article in the newspaper which said that ballet was 'anti-feminist and bourgeois'.

Jessamy wasn't quite sure what bourgeois meant (nor how to pronounce it), but it was obviously a term of abuse. She had shown the article to Karen, who read it slowly with puckered lips, and then said that she wasn't sure, either.

'I think perhaps what they mean is that only well-off people can do it.'

'Well, only well-off people can come to this school!' retorted Jessamy. 'That doesn't seem to bother them. Besides, it's not true. Lots of poor kids get accepted for the Royal Ballet School and Central.'

'Not lots,' said Karen. 'Only a few. It's much easier to get in if you can pay for it.'

Everything was easier if you could pay for it, thought Jessamy. That was a fact of life. 'It isn't our fault if we've got quite well-off parents,' she said.

Two little spots of pink appeared in Karen's cheeks. Her skin was a delicate pale ivory, unlike Jessamy's, which was quite rosy and tended to break out into freckles at the first hint of sunshine.

'Perhaps it's just that people it's made easy for should be grateful and know that it's not the same for everyone.'

'Oh, well, yes. Of *course*.'

Jessamy said of course, but she was not, as a matter of fact, very often grateful for having a famous family. There were even times when she was tempted to think it a positive bore, like, for instance, when they were trying to sit quietly together in a restaurant enjoying a meal and idiot people nearby started staring and pointing and whispering behind their hands. Saul, who was the good-natured one of the family, said that it was 'all part and parcel', but it made Jessamy want to go and poke her fingers in people's eyes.

She accepted, all the same, that Karen was right. She *ought* to be grateful, because it wasn't the same for everyone.

She wondered if it were Karen's parents who had taught her to think like that – like a politician, almost – but when she asked her, Karen shook her head and said that she didn't have any parents.

'They're both dead. My mum died when I was born and my dad died afterwards, in a car crash. I live with my gran.'

Jessamy thought, that would account for the fact that in some ways Karen was strangely old-fashioned. She had never been to a sleep-over, knew almost nothing about pop music (though everything about ballet music), and even at weekends, when everyone else dressed for fun, went round in sweaters and skirts and sensible shoes. Jessamy bumped into her one Saturday afternoon in the library, looking for ballet books.

'I've got stacks of ballet books at home,' said Jessamy. 'I've got all the ones that were my mum and dad's and all the ones that were Saul's and all the ones that were Jack's and all the ones that are mine.'

Ballet books, indeed, filled every available centimetre of shelf space in the Hart household, and then spilled out across the floor.

'Do you want to come back and look at them? You could stay to tea, if you like.'

'*Could* I?' said Karen.

She made it sound as if she were being invited to Buckingham Palace to meet royalty. Jessamy always had to remind herself that in the ballet world the Harts *were* a sort of royalty. Only very minor, of course; nothing compared to the all-time greats. But her dad had been one of the finest Petrushkas in the business until he had developed chronic tendonitis and had to retire, and people even now talked of Belinda Tarrant's Princess Aurora. Even Saul, at only twenty, was dancing leading roles.

'Let's go back and you can look at the books and then it'll be tea time and then we can watch a video.'

'Would it be all right if I telephoned my gran?'

'Of course,' said Jessamy, grandly. 'You can do it from the phone in my bedroom.'

Karen picked out a great pile of books which she wanted to read – she kept asking, 'Is it all right? *Really*?' whenever she discovered that they had 'Ben Hart' or 'Belinda Tarrant' written inside them – and then she and Jessamy went downstairs to ask Elke, the German au pair, if she would do them some tea. They ate their tea with Elke, in the basement kitchen, trying to talk in German to her because you never knew when German might come in useful later on, when they were touring. After that, they went into the sitting-room to watch a video.

'Where are your mum and dad?' said Karen.

'Mum's gone to a conference. Dad's still in New York. What do you want to watch? Would you like to watch *Giselle*? We've got the *best Giselle* – well, I think it's the best. It's Carla Fracci and Erik Bruhn. I always weep buckets when Giselle dies. And Hilarion. I think it's so unfair on Hilarion. After all, he was in love with Giselle long before Albrecht arrived, and he really *was* in love.'

'But so was Albrecht,' pleaded Karen, 'by the end.'

'By the end it's too late. He's already done the damage. That's what comes of princes dressing up and pretending to be peasants.'

When Jessamy had shown the video of *Giselle* to Susan and Sheela they had irritated her by going 'Ooh' and 'Aah' every time anyone got up on their toes or did anything which looked in the least bit complicated. Susan and Sheela had no idea what was difficult and what was relatively easy. Karen was far more knowledgeable. She and Jessamy spent most of the first act passing comments to each other until they reached the mad scene, when they both sat spellbound with tears pouring down their cheeks.

'Carla Fracci is so wonderful,' snuffled Karen. 'And I see what you mean about Hilarion . . . he doesn't deserve to die!'

'Saul says I'm only sorry for him 'cause he's handsome,' said Jessamy, 'but it's not that. It's 'cause he dances it like a real person, not just a Jealous Gamekeeper.'

They watched as poor Hilarion, driven by the implacable Wilis, was finally hounded to death. Shyly, Karen said, 'He looks a bit like your brother.'

'Mm. I s'pose Saul is quite handsome. That's why he gets all these fan letters from people saying they're in love with him.'

'Women?' said Karen.

'And men.'

Karen looked at her, wide-eyed.

'You have to accept these things,' said Jessamy. 'It isn't any good being naive.'

'No.' Karen swallowed. 'Of course not.'

'Look! They're circling! I love this bit.'

The Wilis, victorious, wheeled about the stage and disappeared; and then a grief-stricken Albrecht came into the picture, clasping a bunch of flowers to place on Giselle's grave.

'I can't help feeling a *bit* sorry for Albrecht,' said Karen.

'Yes, 'cause he's Erik Bruhn and he's gorgeous.' Jessamy sighed and blotted contentedly at her eyes. She always cried when she watched *Giselle*. 'Some people say he's the greatest dancer there's ever been . . . even greater than Nureyev.'

Karen looked shocked.

'Who says that?'

'Well, my dad for a start. My mum says she can never make up her mind. She says they had different qualities. I think they're both beautiful.'

'They are.' Karen nodded ecstatically, her handkerchief balled into her hand for the tears that were still to come.

'I adore the second act,' breathed Jessamy. 'It's almost my favourite in all ballet. I wish I could be Giselle!'

'Why can't you?'

'Not the type. You are. You're lucky. Look, that's Toni Lander as the Queen of the Wilis . . . isn't she heaven?'

It was dark by the time they had finished watching *Giselle* so Elke very kindly got the car out to drive Karen home.

'I'll come with you,' said Jessamy.

'You don't have to,' said Karen.

'I want to. There won't be anything else to do after you've gone.'

Watching ballet with a fellow enthusiast was so much more fun than watching it by yourself. She had one or two friends at ballet school, but nobody really close. There was too much rivalry and competition, and everyone was too aware of who she was: the daughter of Belinda Tarrant.

'You must come round again and we'll watch something else,' said Jessamy.

'That would be brilliant,' said Karen. She hesitated. 'I'm sorry I can't invite you back to my place, but my gran's a bit funny about things like that. And anyway,' she added, 'we haven't got a video.'

'That's OK,' said Jessamy. 'You can come to me. It's easier that way . . . I'll show you my collection of shoes next time.'

Jessamy had a whole collection of old ballet shoes, all worn and discarded and signed for her by their owners. Susan and Sheela had wrinkled their noses and said, 'Ugh! They're disgusting! Like old dishrags!' In their simplicity they had thought that ballet shoes lasted for performance after performance and still ended up all lovely and pink and shiny. They had been incredulous when Jessamy told them that quite often they scarcely even lasted for as much as one act.

'That is so *wasteful*,' Susan had said, severely.

What Karen wanted to know was whether Jessamy had one of Rudolph Nureyev's.

'No,' said Jessamy, 'but I've got one of Gelsey Kirkland's . . . You can try it on, if you like.'

Karen sighed, blissfully, as the car drew up outside a row of small terraced houses.

'Ask your gran if you can come next weekend,' said Jessamy.

On Monday, at the end of English, Mrs Richmond asked Jessamy to stay behind.

'Well, now, Jessamy,' she said, 'I take it we can rely on you to come up with something for our end-of-term production, as usual?'

Jessamy's face obviously didn't quite register the enthusiasm that it should have done, for quickly Mrs Richmond added, 'It is one of the high spots, you know. Everyone looks forward to it. The end of term wouldn't be the end of term without a contribution from you. You are, after all, our star performer!'

Jessamy forced herself to beam. It wasn't that she didn't want to dance for them, just that it would have been nice, for once, to be considered as an actress.

'We're doing a rain forest play,' said Mrs Richmond. 'Look, I've brought a copy of the script for you. I thought a short solo at the beginning and another at the end might round things off rather satisfactorily.'

'All right,' said Jessamy. 'I'll think of something.'

That evening, after doing her homework (and after having her ballet class) she nobly sat down to read Mrs Richmond's script. She would far rather have read a ballet book or watched a ballet video, but already, at eleven years old, Jessamy had the outlook of a true professional: if a job had to be done, then get on and do it.

The rain forest play was strange and rather beautiful, full of talking trees and choruses of frogs, but after she had read it Jessamy didn't mind so much about not being considered as an actress. She didn't regard it as acting to play a talking tree or be part of a frog chorus. Acting, to Jessamy, was being people. And even now ideas for her solos were rushing pell-mell into her brain.

The Spirit of the Rain Forest . . . a costume of leaves, deep, dark, shiny green, with a headdress of feathers in vivid parrot colours. Yellow, orange, scarlet . . . her shoes would have to be dyed. Green, probably, with green tights.

Jessamy reached out for a drawing pad. Already she was growing excited. Jack, who had escaped Coombe Hurst productions by starting off somewhere else and then going to the Royal Ballet School at the age of eleven, always dismissed Jessamy's end-of-term solos as 'tacky, if not downright naff'. In her heart of hearts, Jessamy sometimes agreed with her, but as her mum said, 'It's all good preparation . . . the more used to performing you are, the better. And the world needs new choreographers.'

Jessamy wasn't sure that her choreography was anything very amazing, but she did quite enjoy putting different combinations of steps together. Occasionally, if her dad were at home he helped her, but this year she was going to have to manage by herself.

Jessamy put down her pad and walked to the centre of the room. Slowly she went on *demi-pointe* and raised her arms in fifth ... the Spirit of the Rain Forest!

3

Ballonné – extend step forward – *dégagé derrière* and close in fifth.

Jessamy paused to look at herself in the long mirror which she had brought downstairs from mum and dad's bedroom. Critically, she readjusted her weight. That was better; try it again. *Ballonné* –

She had worked out her Rain Forest dance using some music by a composer called Villa-Lobos, which she had found on one of her dad's CDs. The opening sequence lasted three minutes, and the closing sequence five, which she thought was about right. All she had to do now was find time to practise it, and that wasn't so easy. She couldn't stay on at the Academy after class because the studio was needed for other lessons, and the sitting-room, which was where she was at the moment, was really far too small and cluttered even with all the furniture pushed out of the way. In any case, Elke grew grumpy when she had to come and move everything back again.

'I am not here – ' huff puff ' – as a removals person.'

Some of the furniture was quite heavy: Jessamy went scarlet in the face when she tried to push it, so *that* couldn't be good for her.

Last year the sitting-room had been all right because last year she had only been ten and had done a really soppy, yucky sort of number full of silly little hops and skips such as befitted a ten-year-old. The Spirit of the Rain Forest was more ambitious, with proper jumps and even a couple of *pirouettes* (Jessamy rather fancied herself at *pirouettes*).

'I need somewhere to practise!' she moaned, as Elke came tutting into the room.

'Look at all this trouble you make! You move the furniture one more time, I leave it for your mother to see.'

'But I need to *practise*,' wailed Jessamy.

'Practise, practise! All I ever hear in this house,' grumbled Elke. 'Nobody thinks of any one thing but *practise*.'

In the end, Jessamy had an idea: she would go in early to school and practise in the gym. It wasn't easy, getting up early, but once Jessamy had set her mind to do something she always did it.

'Please, Elke, will you bang on my door at half-past six . . . please will you bang really hard?'

'What am I now?' cried Elke. 'An alarm clock person?'

But Elke was always up early. Jessamy had heard her singing pop songs in the bathroom before it was even light.

'Please, Elke!' she said. 'It's very important.'

Her end-of-term solos may be what Jacquetta called tacky, but they still had to be done well.

Next morning, Jessamy was down in the kitchen, washed and dressed and ready for breakfast by seven o'clock. By quarter-past seven Elke was driving her in to school.

'If Mum wants to know where I am,' said Jessamy, 'tell her I've gone in early to do some extra practice.'

The chances were Belinda Tarrant wouldn't even miss her. She was always too busy opening her post and sipping black coffee to notice much of what went on before midday.

Jessamy slipped into school by one of the side doors – opened by the caretaker for those who came in before school for extra music lessons or games practice – and made her way up to the gym. The gym was modern, with a good wood block floor, perfect for dancing. It wasn't until she had pushed open the swing doors that Jessamy made the discovery: someone else had had the same idea!

Karen, dressed in leotard and tights (the same as Jessamy herself under her regulation school blouse and skirt) was there doing *pliés*, using the wall bar to hold on to. She stopped and spun round, her face scarlet, as Jessamy appeared.

'Great minds!' said Jessamy.

'P–pardon?' stammered Karen.

'Great minds think alike . . . I wanted somewhere I could practise my end-of-term solo.'

'That's all right!' Karen snatched up her clothes, which she had draped over the back of one of the horses. 'I was just finishing.'

She obviously hadn't been just finishing: she had been just starting. Jessamy leapt forward, impulsively. 'You don't have to go! Why don't we practise together?'

Karen looked doubtful.

'But if you want to do your solo – '

'Not before I've warmed up,' said Jessamy. She stripped down to her leotard and sat on the floor to put on her shoes. 'Have you used the gym before?'

'Only this week.' Karen said it anxiously. 'I wanted to do some extra work and it was the only place I could think of. Do you think they'll mind?'

'Don't see why they should. It's not as if we're using any of their equipment.' Jessamy gazed round at the gym with its ropes and its wall bars. 'It's a pity there isn't any music ... I might bring my portable CD player!'

'But suppose someone heard us?'

'Who could? There isn't anyone about.' The gym was at the back of the school, on the first floor; the staff room and Miss Shergold's office were both on the ground floor, at the front.

'We've got it all to ourselves! Our own private studio. How far had you got? Just *pliés*?'

They went through *pliés, battements tendus, ronds de jambes, battements frappés, battements fondus, grands battements* and *développés*. Watching Karen, when she could (she couldn't watch herself: the one drawback of the gym was that there were no mirrors for checking your position), Jessamy thought that whoever Madame Olga was and however ancient she might be she had certainly taught her well.

'Are you going to do your solo now?' said Karen.

'What, before we do any centre work?'

Karen looked at the gym clock.

'I don't think there'd be time for both.'

'All right. I'll just run through it quickly and show you what I've worked out ... 'cause I've just had this really great idea,' said Jessamy, taking up her position in the centre of the gym. 'Why don't you learn it as well and we could make it a *pas de deux*?'

'They wouldn't want me doing it,' said Karen.

'Why not?' They could still have the great Jessamy Hart and her famous parents. 'It would be more fun than just me. I'm always doing it. Look! Watch and tell me what you think.'

Fortunately, Jessamy knew the music so well that she could hear it in her head as she danced. Karen sat quietly watching her.

'There!' said Jessamy. 'It's not terribly good yet, but that's what I'm planning to do. What d'you think?'

'I think it's brilliant,' said Karen.

'Really? Really and truly? You're not just saying it?'

'No, I mean it. That bit where you – ' Karen stood up and demonstrated. 'That works really well.'

'The *pas de chat*. I worked on that for ages. I couldn't get it to fit in properly.'

'It looks really good.'

'Yes, because it's a bit showy.' A bit showy, but actually quite simple to do. 'Like the *pirouettes*. They always like *pirouettes*. I wish I could do them on point! Have you gone on point yet?'

Karen shook her head.

'Madame says it's too early.'

'Yes, that's what Mum says. She says not until my feet are stronger. *I* think they're strong enough now.' Jessamy wriggled her toes inside their soft shoes. 'I'm really looking forward to buying my first point shoes. Aren't you? You don't feel you've properly started until you can wear point shoes.'

'I expect our toes will get sore,' said Karen.

'Jack's always used to bleed. She used to try stuffing things in her shoes to make it easier. Have you got good feet for point work?'

'Quite,' said Karen. She took off a shoe and displayed her toes: the first and second ones were the same length.

'Look at mine,' said Jessamy. She wasn't boasting: she just happened to have been blessed with good strong feet and ankles, and three toes the same length on each foot.

Karen sighed. 'You are so lucky,' she said.

'I know. I bet I could go on point right now if only Mum wasn't so pernickety. Anyway –' Jessamy stuffed her ballet shoes back into their bag and pulled on her ordinary brown lace-ups. 'What do you think about us doing a *pas de deux*?'

Karen, still sitting on the floor, pressed the soles of her feet together. She bent her head over them.

'I don't think Madame would let me. She's very strict about things like that.'

'But it's good for you!' said Jessamy. 'It gives you experience of being on stage.'

'Y–yes, I know, but – '

'Why don't you give me her telephone number and I'll get Mum to ring her? I bet she'd be able to talk her round! Mum says it's important for a dancer to get the feel of performing. She says if you just slog away in class all the time you get stale, Which is quite true,' said Jessamy. 'Doesn't your madame ever let you do performances?'

Slowly, Karen straightened up.

40

'It's not so much Madame, it's – it's more my gran. She wouldn't like it. She's funny about things like that.'

Jessamy frowned. Karen's gran seemed to be a very strange person, being 'funny' about things all the time. She was funny about Karen inviting friends home, funny about Karen performing on stage –

'She's a bit old-fashioned.'

Karen said it apologetically. Jessamy could see that it was difficult for her. Jessamy herself didn't have any grandparents. They had all died when she was still quite young. But once there had been a girl at school who was a member of the Plymouth Brethren and *her* parents hadn't ever let her join in with after-school activities, so Jessamy knew that these sort of people did exist.

'Is your gran a Plymouth Brother?' she said.

'What's a Plymouth Brother?' said Karen.

'A sort of religious person . . . very strict.'

Karen grew red and shook her head. 'No, my gran isn't like that. She's just . . . just old-fashioned.'

'Well, it's a shame,' said Jessamy. 'It would have been fun, dancing together. But if it's something that would really upset her – '

'It would,' said Karen.

Jessamy paused in the middle of tying her school tie.

'What's she going to do when you go to ballet school? You'll have to do performances then.'

Karen looked at Jessamy, gravely.

'I don't yet know whether she'll let me.'

'But that's *terrible*!' said Jessamy.

'I know.' Karen's eyes filled with sudden tears. She

dashed them away and began peeling off her leotard. 'We'd better hurry or we'll be late for assembly!'

When once Jessamy took an idea into her head, she did not part with it easily. Karen *ought* to join her in the Rain Forest dance. It was sickmaking, Jessamy hogging the limelight every year just because she was the daughter of Ben Hart and Belinda Tarrant. And it was appalling if Karen's gran wouldn't let her become a dancer! Every morning now, the two girls met in the gym to do half an hour of class and to practise the Rain Forest dance – well, Jessamy practised the Rain Forest dance. Karen just shook her head when Jessamy suggested she should practise it with her.

'There isn't any point. I wouldn't be allowed.'

Something, thought Jessamy, would have to be done. She had seen enough of Karen's dancing to know that she had talent, and Jessamy had been brought up in a family which firmly believed that talent should not be wasted. They believed this as fervently as some people believed in God. Indeed, to them talent *was* a god – which was why they had been so angry with Jacquetta for tossing hers aside just as carelessly as if it had been an old glove or some worn-out article of clothing.

'Sacrilege!' had cried Jessamy's mum.

Jessamy wasn't absolutely certain what sacrilege was, but she believed just as firmly as the rest of the family (with the exception of Jack) that talent should be put to good use. Karen's talent, it seemed to her, was being stifled. Probably Karen's gran didn't realise that it wasn't something that could survive being shut up within four walls. It needed to expand; it needed to

42

breathe. If Jessamy went round and explained this to her – very politely, of course – then surely she would see?

Jessamy made up her mind. She wouldn't tell Karen what she was planning to do, because Karen mightn't like it (though she would be eternally grateful afterwards), but on Wednesday, which was the day she didn't have a ballet class after school, she told Elke not to bother coming to pick her up.

'I'm going round to Susan's for a bit.'

'So I come and pick you up later from Susan's?'

'No, it's all right,' said Jessamy. 'I'll catch a bus.'

Elke raised her eyebrows.

'It may by then be after dark. Your mother will not like for you to be out after dark. I come for you.'

Really, thought Jessamy, trying to hatch plots and do things without other people knowing was extraordinarily difficult when you were only eleven years old.

'You say what time,' said Elke.

It wasn't any use arguing. Elke might object to moving furniture around, but she took her official duties very seriously.

'I'll give you a call when I'm leaving,' said Jessamy.

Susan didn't live too far away from Karen. She would go round to Susan's place and telephone from there. And it probably *wouldn't* be after dark. How long would it take to convince Karen's gran that Karen needed to dance? Five minutes? Ten minutes? Jessamy had great faith in her own powers of persuasion.

She walked out of school with Karen, who was, as usual, going to Madame Olga's. Karen turned left. Jessamy waited a moment, then turned right, in the direction of the buses. She knew how to get to Bolton Street, which was where Karen's gran lived: she had looked it up in the *A-Z*.

Quarter of an hour later, she was knocking at the door of Number Fifteen. Anyone else might have felt a little nervous perhaps, but not Jessamy. Overweening confidence was what Jessamy had (her brother Saul had said so).

The door opened on to a long, dark, narrow passage. A little old lady stood there. She was tiny – hardly any taller than Jessamy – thin as a twig, and fragile like a bird. She was wearing slippers, and a flowered pinafore and was drying her hands on a towel.

'Good afternoon,' said Jessamy, in her best imitation of her mum. 'My name is Jessamy Hart. I'm a friend of Karen's. Are you Karen's gran?'

'Yes, my dear. What can I do for you? I'm afraid Karen's not here at the moment. She never gets back until about five.'

'I know,' said Jessamy. 'That's why I came, so we could talk on our own.'

'Oh.' Karen's gran sounded rather flustered. 'Oh! Well! You'd better come in.' She held the door open and Jessamy stepped through into the narrow hallway. 'Go into the front room, Jessamy . . . take a seat. Now, what was it you wanted to talk about?'

'It's about Karen dancing in the end-of-term show.'

'Karen dancing in the end-of-term show?' Her gran's face lit up. 'Oh! That is nice!'

Jessamy was thrown.

'You mean you don't mind?' she said.

'Mind? Of course I don't mind. I'm only too happy

for her. I always feel a bit guilty, to tell you the truth, about Karen and her dancing. Obsessed with it, she is. I keep hoping it's just a passing phase – we all have passing phases, don't we, when we're young? I remember for years I most passionately wanted to be a jockey and ride in the Grand National. Oh, dear! And we never had the money for a single riding lesson. But it didn't stop me dreaming. A bit like Karen, I'm afraid. She obviously takes after her gran.'

Jessamy listened with growing bewilderment. The conversation was not following at all the course she had planned. By now she should have been in full flood, exercising her powers of persuasion.

'So you really wouldn't mind,' she said, 'if Karen danced in the show?'

'So long as it's not going to put too much pressure on her. The only thing that bothers me is whether she would have enough time. What with all these extra bits and pieces she has to stay behind for – '

Extra bits and pieces? Jessamy wrinkled her brow.

'What extra bits and pieces?'

'Oh! I don't know. Netball, is it? Or gym? Something she has to do. And then there's some special class she has to stay on for twice a week . . . never home before five o'clock. They do seem to work you very hard at that school.'

Jessamy didn't know what to say. What were these special classes supposed to be? She wondered for a truly dreadful minute if Karen's gran were not quite right in the head. Maybe she was growing forgetful, as old people sometimes did, and it had slipped her

45

memory that Karen had ballet lessons every afternoon with Madame Olga.

'Not that I'm complaining,' said Karen's gran. 'Don't think that! It's what her granddad always wanted for her. He was never lucky enough to have an education himself, but he was determined that Karen should. Dreamt of her going to university, he did. I don't know whether she'll get that far.'

Karen's gran broke off and cocked a hopeful eye in Jessamy's direction. Jessamy, who was never at a loss for words, said, 'Um – well – ' and was then at a loss. To herself she thought, not at Coombe Hurst, she won't. Coombe Hurst was not noted for its academic success. You went to the High School if you wanted that. Portia, probably, would transfer to the High School before very long. She was far too much of a genius for Coombe Hurst.

Karen's gran, as if reading Jessamy's mind, said, 'We tried for the High School, but she wasn't quite up to it. Too much dreaming about ballet, I put it down to.' Jessamy watched as the old woman pleated the edge of her apron with gnarled fingers. 'She's always pleading with me, but what can I do? When her grandad said education he meant book learning, not ballet. It wouldn't be right to use the money for dancing. Not when he worked so hard for it.'

'But what about – about Madame Olga?' The question was out before Jessamy could stop it.

'Madame Olga?' Karen's gran looked at her, blankly. She had the same blue eyes as Karen, only slightly cloudy now because of her being old. 'That'll be one of her dancers, I suppose. All over her bedroom, they

46

are ... Margaret Fonteyn, that Nooryeff. I can't keep up with them. I don't know where she gets it from, there's no ballet in the family. Mind you, her mother was musical; that might have something to do with it. But you can tell her – well, I'll tell her when she gets in. I've no objections to her dancing in the show so long as her school work doesn't suffer.'

'Actually – ' Jessamy stood up, suddenly anxious to be away. It had all gone most peculiarly wrong! 'Actually, would you mind terribly *not* telling her that I came? She might think I've been spying on her, or something.'

'Well, of course you haven't!' Karen's gran sounded indignant. 'You were just being normally friendly. I must say I'm very glad to have met one of Karen's friends at last. I keep asking her, why don't you bring someone home with you? All she does is make excuses. I hope she's not becoming too big for her boots, going to this posh school?'

'I'm sure she isn't,' said Jessamy, doing her best to slide out of the front door.

'You don't think she's ashamed of her old gran, do you?'

'I'm *sure* she isn't!' gasped Jessamy.

Karen wasn't ashamed of her gran. She was terrified that someone would discover her secret: that she was having lessons every afternoon with Madame Olga and that her gran didn't know! The mystery of it was, how was she managing to pay?

'Ask her to bring you to tea,' called her gran, as Jessamy opened the front gate.

'I will,' promised Jessamy.

She would, but she knew what Karen would say: 'My gran doesn't like me having people back. She's a bit funny like that . . .'

4

There was a mystery about Karen. You wouldn't have thought it to look at her, with her shy smile and demure manner, but she was obviously something of a dark horse. There was more to her, thought Jessamy, than met the eye, and one of these days she was going to discover what it was.

In the meantime, it had now become almost taken for granted that Jessamy and Elke would go and fetch her in the car after lunch on Saturday – Karen's gran didn't have a car – and that Karen would stay to tea and watch ballet videos, or look at Jessamy's collections of shoes and signed photographs. Karen had been gratifyingly impressed to find that she actually had a signed photograph of Rudolph Nureyev. (Even Susan and Sheela had heard of Rudolph Nureyev.)

'Mum got it for me,' said Jessamy.

'Did she ever dance with him?'

'Well, she wasn't actually partnered by him, but they danced on the same stage.'

'Did you ever meet him?'

'Oh, yes,' said Jessamy, airily. 'Several times.'

Karen's eyes grew big and round.

'*Really*? What was he like?'

Jessamy struggled for a moment. It would be easy

enough to say 'nice', or 'funny', or 'friendly', but the truth was she didn't actually know. She giggled.

'I can't remember . . . I was only two years old!' She only knew about it because the family never tired of reminding her.

'At least you can say that you've met him,' sighed Karen. 'I've never met anyone great.' And then she blushed and added, 'Of course, you're used to it, with your mum and dad.'

'Mum and Dad aren't great like Nureyev was. Mum always says Rudi was in a class of his own . . . do you want to watch one of his videos? I've got one of him and Fonteyn. Shall we look at that?'

Karen nodded, blissfully. She couldn't have enough of watching ballet. She had already confessed to Jessamy that the only ballet she had ever seen live, on stage, was *Swan Lake*, which her gran had taken her to as a treat on her birthday.

'We'll go together, in the holidays,' promised Jessamy. 'Saul can get me free tickets sometimes.' She pressed the start switch on the remote control. 'Look! This is *Don Quixote*. Later there's the balcony scene from *Romeo and Juliet*, and then some of *Sylphides*, and then a bit from *Le Corsaire* . . . he's absolutely brilliant in *Le Corsaire*!'

They watched intently, Jessamy curled up into one corner of the sofa, Karen in the other, as Nureyev leapt and spun and bounded in great pantherine leaps across the stage. When he jumped, it was as if invisible hands held him aloft; when he turned, it was as if he were a coiled spring, or a top, unwinding. Jessamy was rather good at turns herself, but even she could only look and wonder. She *knew* how you could spin and spin and not grow dizzy; and yet the speed at which Nureyev did it seemed to defy all the laws of the human body. It simply wasn't possible that anyone could turn so fast for so long – but there he was, in front of them, young and arrogant and insolently beautiful, hair flying out and a smile on his lips as if it were a mere nothing.

Karen let out her breath in a deep sigh of ecstasy.

'He *was* the greatest, wasn't he?'

'He had animal magnetism,' said Jessamy. (It was a phrase she had read somewhere.) 'There'll never be another like him.'

Karen sighed again. So did Jessamy. A tear rolled down Karen's cheek.

'It's so awful that he's not here any more!'

'I know.' Jessamy nodded, solemnly. 'But at least,' she quoted her mum, 'at least his dancing days were over.'

'That's a terrible thing to say!' sobbed Karen.

'But it's true,' insisted Jessamy. She groped for her handkerchief. 'Think of the tragedy if he'd been young!'

'It's a tragedy anyw–way,' wept Karen.

'Oh, don't, I can't bear it!' cried Jessamy.

They were still sitting there, their handkerchiefs pressed to their faces, when the door opened and Saul's head appeared.

'What's this, then?' He jerked a thumb towards the television. 'One for the ghouls?'

'Shut up,' said Jessamy. 'Don't be beastly.'

'I'm not being beastly.' Saul crossed to the back of the sofa and leant over, between the two of them, watching as the dazzling figure of Le Corsaire soared, bare-chested and triumphant, through the air, curving and curling like a great golden eagle in effortless flight.

For a long while there was silence, then, 'By God, he was good!' said Saul.

'The greatest,' said Jessamy, scrubbing at her eyes.

'Certainly one of.'

'*The* greatest. Karen thinks so.'

Karen's face, still awash with tears, promptly turned itself into a glowing beacon.

'Karen thinks so, does she?' Saul cocked an eye, considering her. 'Well, she could be right. I'll tell you one thing . . . none of us could hold a candle to him.'

'He transformed the face of British ballet,' said Jessamy.

'He did. That's for sure.'

'Before Nureyev,' said Jessamy, 'idiot ordinary people thought that male dancers were soft. He made them realise you had to be a whole lot tougher than stupid footballers.'

'You bet!' said Saul. He straightened up. 'Well, I'll leave you to it.'

Jessamy turned to watch him go.

'Why are you home?' she said. 'Aren't you on tonight?'

'Knee injury. I'm out for a couple of days.'

'If you were any sort of a dancer,' yelled Jessamy, as Saul limped elaborately across the room, 'you'd dance through it!'

'Yeah, and cripple myself?' retorted Saul.

The sitting-room door closed behind him.

'Getting soft,' said Jessamy. The video had come to

an end. She pressed the rewind button. 'That was my brother, by the way,' she said.

'I know!' Karen's face was still all aglow with pink.

'Fancy stopping dancing just for a knee injury!' Jessamy said it scornfully. 'I wouldn't.'

'You'd have to if it were bad.'

'Nureyev didn't,' said Jessamy. 'He danced through anything. So did all Balanchine's dancers. They *suffered* for their art. Gelsey Kirkland had tendonitis when she was only twelve years old.'

Karen looked at her, doubtfully.

'That sounds like bad training,' she said.

'Yes, he used to push them. Mum says he was a tyrant, but everyone worshipped him. What shall we watch next?' Jessamy went on hands and knees, scrabbling through a pile of videos. 'I've got one of Mum here. Do you want to see one of Mum? Or there's a bit of Dad, but it's not very good. It's a pirate version. Someone taped it when they shouldn't have. Let's look at Mum.'

'You're ever so like him,' said Karen.

'Who?' Jessamy sat back on her heels. 'Saul?'

She knew that she was like him for everyone was always telling her so – Karen herself had remarked on it even before she had met him. Jessamy really should have been used to it by now, but still she couldn't quite stop a pleased beam from spreading itself over her face.

Only last week, in a review, Saul had been described as 'this handsome and talented young dancer'. Of course, Mum and Jacquetta were the real *beauties* in the family; but if she grew up to look like a female version of Saul she wouldn't mind. *Jessamy Hart, this handsome and talented young dancer* ...

'You are so lucky,' said Karen.

Karen was always saying that Jessamy was lucky. She didn't say it at all in an envious sort of way, though sometimes she sounded wistful, as if she would have liked parents who belonged to the world of ballet and understood the urgent need to express oneself in dance. Jessamy, who had always tended to take her ballet background for granted, was beginning to see that perhaps she *was* rather more fortunate than others. It must be truly devastating, for instance, to have as much talent as Karen and to live with a gran who insisted that education meant book learning and not ballet.

On the other hand, Karen was actually having more lessons than Jessamy, and private lessons at that, so perhaps she needn't feel too sorry for her.

'There are drawbacks,' said Jessamy, 'to having parents that are dancers.'

'I'd give *any*thing,' said Karen.

'You wouldn't if you had to have lessons from your own mother and she was always holding you up as an example of how not to do things and expecting you to work twice as hard as anyone else and get better exam results than anyone else and fussing all the time about whether your feet are strong enough and how tall you're likely to grow and –'

Karen listened with shining eyes.

'You wouldn't think it so much fun then,' grumbled Jessamy.

'I would!' said Karen. 'I'd love it!'

Jessamy looked at her. She shook her head.

'You are bananas,' she said. 'Ballet bananas!'

'I've had an idea!' announced Jessamy, bounding into the gym one morning.

She and Karen always met there now, before school, just as they spent every Saturday afternoon together, though during the day Jessamy still went round with Susan and Sheela, while Karen and Portia stuck with each other. Jessamy suspected that quite soon – next term, maybe, if Portia transferred to the High – Karen would move in to make a foursome; and within the foursome it would be Susan-and-Sheela, and Karen-and-Jessamy; but for the moment none of the others realised how much time they spent together out of school hours. It was good to have someone to talk to who spoke the same language. Jessamy could confide things to Karen that she could never confide to the girls at ballet school – her growing certainty, for example, that she was going to turn into a dramatic dancer rather than a classical one. The girls at ballet school would immediately have latched on.

'Of course, *she*'s never going to dance the lead in *Swan Lake*. She might think she's the cat's whiskers just because of who her parents are, but it won't get her anywhere – not in the long run.'

All Karen said, very seriously, was 'But, Jessamy, some of the *best* dancers have been dramatic . . . look at Lynn Seymour!' And Jessamy did, and took comfort, and became a bit reconciled. After all, Lynn Seymour had danced with Rudolph Nureyev.

'Look,' she said now, as she burst through the swing doors into the gym, 'why don't I give you a class and then you give me a class and then we can tell each other all our faults?'

Karen looked dubious. 'Is that a good idea?'

'I think so,' said Jessamy.

It was all part of a cunning ploy to find out more about Madame Olga. Jessamy had several times in her life been accused of being pushy, but even she didn't quite like to ask outright, 'Where are you getting the money to pay for your ballet lessons?' Perhaps Madame Olga was giving them free because Karen had such obvious talent; or perhaps Karen had discovered a secret hoard of money under her bedroom floorboards – well, no, she didn't seriously think that; that was the sort of stuff that story books were made of. All the same, there *was* a mystery and Jessamy wasn't going to rest until she had got to the bottom of it.

'Come on!' she said. 'Let's get started.'

'But what about your Rain Forest dance?'

'I don't have to do it every day. Now, come along, please!' Jessamy clapped her hands, as Mum sometimes did at the beginning of class. 'At the *barre*! *Pliés* in first.'

She pressed the start button on her portable CD player. Karen obediently took up her position at the wall bars.

'And one, and two – '

Try as she might, Jessamy couldn't find a single thing to criticise in Karen's *barre* work.

'Your *développés* could be just a *teeny* bit smoother.' But really that was just nitpicking; not even Belinda Tarrant would have found fault with Karen's *développés*. Jessamy was only saying it for the sake of something to say. 'Just a teensy weensy bit. You'll have to work on it. OK, my turn!'

Jessamy sprang across to take her place.

'You can say what you like,' she said. 'I won't be offended.'

She wasn't really expecting Karen to say anything. After all, Jessamy had been taking dancing classes since she was five years old; far longer than Karen.

'Well?' As she reached the last of her *développés* – as smooth as smooth could be – she turned, challengingly, to Karen. 'How was that?'

'Very good,' said Karen, 'on the whole.'

Very good *on the whole*? Jessamy bristled.

'What was wrong?'

'Nothing very much.' Karen said it soothingly. 'I just felt now and again that you were straining your neck just a little bit.'

Jessamy's cheeks grew red with indignation. Who did Karen Anders think she was, telling Jessamy Hart that she was straining her neck?

'I'm sorry,' said Karen, 'but you did say to tell you.'

Yes, and it was no more than her mum had pointed out to her last week, was it?

'You must take care, Jessamy, not to strain your neck . . . there's nothing worse than someone dancing with her head all poked forward.'

'It's 'cause my neck isn't as long and beautiful as yours.' Jessamy felt suddenly generous. 'I always feel I have to stretch it.'

'There isn't any need,' said Karen, 'honestly! It's a perfectly good sort of neck.'

Jessamy had to subdue an instinctive dancer's reaction to rush to the nearest mirror and look.

'Well, I suppose it will have to do,' she said, 'as it's the only one I've got . . . Your Madame has taught you really well. Does she have lots of other pupils besides you?'

'Um – not really.' Karen busied herself with the CD player. 'Just one or two.'

'How did you find her?'

'Oh . . . someone told me about her. Someone at my old school.'

'Someone who'd been with her?'

'No, someone who – who lived near her.'

'In Chiswick?'

'Mm.'

Slyly, thinking herself clever, Jessamy said, 'I suppose your gran had to go with you when you auditioned?'

Karen made a mumbling sound: not quite yes and not quite no.

'It must cost a lot,' said Jessamy, 'having classes every day.'

Karen made another mumbling sound. This time, she was pulling her brown school sweater over her head.

'I'd like classes every day,' said Jessamy, 'but Mum says not till next year. I think that's silly, 'cause if I were at ballet school full time I'd be having them.'

'Why aren't you?' said Karen.

Too late, Jessamy realised: she had let herself be sidetracked.

'Mum's scared I'll do a Jack on her. Jack was at White Lodge by the time she was eleven.' She didn't need to explain to Karen that White Lodge was the

Junior Department of the Royal Ballet School: Karen knew these things just as well as Jessamy. 'Mum always reckons she resented it 'cause of never having had any other sort of life except ballet. She says she wants me to be old enough to make up my own mind. Maybe when I'm thirteen she'll let me go.'

'Did your brother go?' said Karen, blushing slightly as she said it.

Jessamy thought, ho ho, she's getting a thing about Saul! She recognised the symptoms. She had seen it too often before: lots of girls had a thing about Saul.

'No,' said Jessamy, 'Saul went to Central. But Saul was different. He was fanatical from the word go. Mum says looking back on it she thinks she pushed Jack too hard. She says I'm half way between them. I'm more dedicated than Jack, but not as fanatical as Saul. Do you think you're fanatical? I mean, is there anything else you'd want to do other than dance?'

'Nothing,' said Karen. She said it in tones of almost tragic intensity. 'If I couldn't dance, I might just as well be dead.'

Jessamy nodded. 'You're like Saul; you're fanatical. I know you wouldn't *think* he's fanatical, all the fuss he makes about a silly little knee injury that anyone else would dance through, but it's because he can't bear the thought of having to give up early, like Dad did.'

'That would be *awful*,' said Karen. 'I'd die if I had to stop dancing.'

'I wouldn't,' said Jessamy. 'I mean, I wouldn't want to, but I'd still go on living.'

59

'But it wouldn't *be* living!' cried Karen. 'Dancing's like breathing. How can you live if you can't breathe?'

Jessamy looked at her, curiously.

'So what will you do if your gran won't let you go to ballet school?'

'I'll find a way.' Karen said it, for her, quite fiercely. 'If you want something badly enough, there's always a way.'

Jessamy thought, I am not very good as a detective. She was no nearer solving the mystery of Karen and Madame Olga than she had been before. There was only one thing for it: direct action was needed.

On Wednesday she said to Elke, 'I'm going to Susan's again. But I'll be back ages before it's dark so I can easily get a bus. You don't have to worry about me.'

'Your mother – ' began Elke.

Jessamy felt like screaming.

'Elke, I'm *eleven*,' she said. 'Loads of people that are eleven go home from school by bus!'

Elke pursed her lips.

'And the main road?' she said.

'I know how to cross the main road!'

Not even Karen's gran fussed and bothered the way Elke did.

'You must ask your mother,' said Elke. 'I take no responsibility.'

Belinda Tarrant, as usual, was busy when Jessamy tried to talk to her.

'Don't bother me now, Jess,' she said.

'So it's OK, is it?' said Jessamy. 'Elke doesn't have to bother getting the car out?'

'Elke doesn't have to do anything she doesn't want to do. She's not here for your personal convenience. She already does far more than she's supposed to.'

Jubilantly, Jessamy reported back: 'Mum says you're not here for my personal convenience and you already do more than you're supposed to.'

Elke's forehead went into a confusion of ripples. 'But it is part of my terms of employment! To call for you from school – '

'Not all the time,' said Jessamy. 'Not on Wednesday. Mum says so.'

The fact that Mum hadn't been listening was neither here nor there. Jessamy had to have *some* freedom of movement. How could she be a detective with Elke dogging her footsteps?

That afternoon, at the end of school, feeling partly like a private detective engaged on a case and partly like a nasty common-or-garden snooper (but whatever she found out she would never let on that she knew) Jessamy raced through the school gates and positioned herself behind a conveniently parked car to wait for Karen to appear. There was a bad moment when Susan and Sheela's grinning faces came looming round the back bumper, demanding to know 'What on earth are you doing *there*?', but she soon despatched them.

'I'm spying on Elke,' she said. 'I think she has a boyfriend.'

'Ooh! Can we spy too?' said Sheela.

'No, it would be too obvious. Go away.'

Giggling, they did so. Seconds later, Karen came through the gates and turned left along Rosemary

Avenue. Jessamy counted up to ten, then crept out after her.

There wasn't any cover in Rosemary Avenue, but fortunately Karen soon turned out of it into Fairhall Road, which was full of shops that could be looked into, and cars that could be hidden behind, and people who sometimes got in the way and obscured your view but also served as camouflage.

Fairhall Road was a long one. If you walked along it one way you eventually came to Hammersmith; if you walked along it the other way you came to a horrible great motorway. Karen was walking in the direction of the motorway.

After a while the shops stopped and the houses started. Some of the houses had been turned into flats and some were empty, with boards nailed across the windows. Karen came to a halt at one of the ones which had boards nailed across it. Jessamy, lingering behind a pillar box, watched in amazement as Karen, after looking quickly to left and right, opened the front gate, walked up the front path, went through a side gate and disappeared.

Now Jessamy wasn't sure what to do. A real detective would have had field glasses, so that she could spy without being seen – except that not even field glasses could penetrate windows which had boards nailed across them. What would a real detective do?

Follow cautiously, thought Jessamy.

She stepped out from behind her pillar box and walked up to the gate. There was a faded sign over the front door which said THE NORAN SCHOOL OF DANCING. Jessamy remembered the Noran School. It had been run by two women called Nora Kline and Annette Pearson, and when it had closed down some of their pupils had transferred to Belinda Tarrant (the ones that were good enough). That had been almost two years ago; the house had obviously been empty ever since. What was Karen going into an empty house for?

Maybe Madame Olga had bought it and hadn't had enough money to put up a new sign. But surely she would at least have taken the boards away from the windows?

Jessamy crept round to the side gate, gently eased it open and slipped through into a dank, dark passage which ran between the Noran School and the house next door. The passage smelt of gunge and stagnant water. Somewhere a tap had overflowed and left a trail of green slime down the wall. At the end of the passage some kind of prickly bush had gone mad and tried to grow all over everything. Carefully, Jessamy picked her way through.

As she emerged from the coils of the prickly bush, she heard the sound of music. So this *was* where Madame Olga held her classes! What a very strange woman she must be.

Jessamy followed the music round to the back of the house. It was coming from a room with windows overlooking the back garden (what *had* been the back garden: it was more of a jungle, now) and double doors opening on to a paved area. Jessamy stood listening for a moment before risking a quick glance through one of the windows. What she saw so astonished her that it was a moment or two before she could bring herself to look again.

The room had evidently been the main studio of the Noran School. There were *barres* still attached to two of the walls, with mirrors along just one of them. At some time there had probably been *barres* and mirrors along the others as well, but now there were just gashes and areas of crumbling plasterwork.

Down the side of the wall, the outside wall by the passage, there was more of the yucky green slime. Beneath it, the floor looked boggy and spongy, while above it, part of the ceiling bellied out like a big water-logged balloon.

And holding on to the *barre*, as far away from the green slime as she could get, was a small figure in leotard and tights. It was Karen. No Madame Olga. Just Karen on her own.

Mesmerised, Jessamy stood on tiptoe, peering through the window as Karen put herself through her *barre* work. At the end of the *barre* work she moved out to the middle of the floor to begin centre practice. Jessamy continued to stand on tiptoe. She almost forgot that she wasn't watching a real class. She wouldn't have been in the least surprised to hear the voice of Madame Olga calling out instructions.

And then Karen stopped, and walked across the room to where she had left her clothes in a heap on top of her school bag, next to a small cassette player from which the music was coming. From the bag she took a book, which she opened at a marked page and spread flat on the floor. She squatted a while on her heels, studying it, then stood up, moved back to the centre of the floor, prepared herself in fifth – and attempted a *pirouette*. Not very successfully. Again she tried, and again. The third time she almost had it, but ended off balance and not quite facing in the right direction.

Jessamy could see where she was going wrong. To begin with, she wasn't spotting properly. She was trying to, Jessamy could tell. She was fixing her eyes on a point somewhere in the middle of the green gunge, but because her head wasn't swinging round fast enough, she kept losing it. Her body was arriving first, leaving her head to follow; that was the problem. Jessamy longed to wrench open the double doors and go running in to set her right, but she knew that she mustn't.

She watched in anguish for a few seconds longer and then could bear it no more. It upset her to see Karen, always so graceful, always so precise, making such a hash of something which really and truly was quite simple – well, Jessamy had always found it so. But then Jessamy had not had to teach herself.

Thoughtfully, she picked her way back round the side of the house, past the prickly bush, down the dank and dingy passage, and up Fairhall Road to the nearest bus stop. No wonder her mum had never heard of Madame Olga. There was no Madame Olga! Everything that Karen knew, she had taught herself. It explained why she hadn't wanted to join Jessamy in the Rain Forest dance, with its couple of showing-off *pirouettes*: she would have had to admit that *pirouettes* were something she had not yet mastered. But I could have taught her! thought Jessamy. I could still teach her – if only she would let me.

She had solved the mystery of Karen's ballet classes, but solving the mystery had created a problem, for how could she offer to help without betraying the fact that she knew? There had to be some way, she thought. Karen was never going to get to grips with those *pirouettes* if someone didn't explain where she was going wrong; and who else was there but Jessamy?

5

'Mum,' said Jessamy, 'do you think it's possible for someone to learn ballet without having a teacher?'

'Of course it isn't,' said her mum. 'What on earth are you talking about?'

'Well, could a person teach herself?'

'No.' Belinda Tarrant was very firm on the point. 'A person could not.'

'Hasn't anyone ever?'

'Not to my knowledge.'

'So maybe they actually *could*?'

'Rubbish! They'd get into all sorts of bad habits.'

Jacquetta, who had drifted up to town on one of her rare visits from the depths of the countryside, which was where she now buried herself in domestic bliss, leaned back amongst the sofa cushions and contentedly swung her legs up on to a footstool.

'You have to remember,' she said, 'that there is a vested interest at stake here.'

'What's a vested interest?' said Jessamy.

'Mum being a teacher . . . she's hardly very likely to admit that she might be disposable.'

Belinda Tarrant snorted. Jacquetta smiled happily and folded her hands over her stomach. Sometimes Jessamy thought that Jacquetta went out of her way to do and say things just to make Mum mad, like this baby she was having. She bet she'd only done it as a gesture of defiance. Who, after all, in their right senses, would want to go round having babies when they could be dancing? Jessamy privately suspected she'd only got married for the same reason. Jacquetta's husband was short and dumpy and fifteen years older than Jacquetta. He was called Neville (stupid name) and he owned a company that made bottles. Mum always referred to him as 'the Bottler'. He had a lot of money, but he didn't know a thing about ballet. What on earth did they find to talk about?

'You don't think,' said Jessamy, 'that if you bought a book which told you how to do all the steps, and if you followed it really *carefully* – '

'You would end up with every fault under the sun.'

Jessamy considered. As far as she could see, Karen didn't have any faults at all – unlike some of the pupils at the Academy. After three years of tuition Lisa Marlowe still hadn't achieved a proper turnout, and probably never would. As Belinda Tarrant said, 'You couldn't make a tutu out of a piece of old rag.'

'You might just about manage to stagger through a few simple *barre* exercises, but after that you'd soon come unstuck.'

Jessamy sighed. 'I suppose so.' It was true that Karen *was* having difficulties with her *pirouettes*.

'Why, anyway?' said Jacquetta.

'I was just wondering.'

'Thinking of branching out on your own?'

'No! Not me. Someone else. They can't afford lessons and they've been trying to teach themself.'

'Can't be done.' Belinda Tarrant spoke briskly. 'A sure recipe for disaster.'

'So what can she do?' wailed Jessamy.

She waited for her mum to say, 'Well, she could come and see me and if she's good enough I might offer to take her on for nothing', but Belinda Tarrant was a professional. She was in business to make money.

'I am not,' as she had more than once rather crisply informed those mothers who had come to her with their mostly untalented daughters begging for favoured treatment, 'a charity institution'.

'What's she supposed to *do*?' demanded Jessamy.

'There are such things as scholarships. The Royal Ballet School, Central – '

'Yes, and how many people get offered them?' In any case, Karen's gran would never let her. She wanted Karen to have book learning.

'If a person has outstanding talent, it will not go unremarked.'

'Yes, but what about all the people with just ordinary talent that can afford to pay? *They* get to have lessons. They don't have to pass scholarships. It isn't fair!' cried Jessamy.

'Did anyone ever say that it was?' Jacquetta swung her legs down off the stool. 'Ballet, my dear Jess, is an élitist art.'

'No more so than anything else!' snapped Belinda Tarrant. She didn't like it when people said that only rich kids could afford to dance. Jessamy had never thought about it before, but she began to see that it was true. She bet there weren't many poor kids at the Royal Ballet School or Central.

'It's the way of the world, kiddo.' Jacquetta turned, and plumped up a cushion. 'Don't let it bug you – there's nothing you can do about it.'

There might not be anything she could do about the world in general, but there must be something, she thought, that she could do for Karen. She racked her brains trying to fathom a way that she could help her without letting on that she had discovered her secret. Karen would feel humiliated if she knew that Jessamy knew. It would be embarrassing, after all the stories she had spun about Madame Olga.

Jessamy thought it quite likely that in Karen's mind Madame Olga really existed. Once when Jessamy had been young and wanted a dog and hadn't been allowed to have one, she made one up. He had been called Toby and he had gone everywhere with her, even, occasionally, to school. If Toby had seemed real, she couldn't see any reason why Madame Olga shouldn't, which meant that Karen hadn't been telling fibs so much as living out a dream. Jessamy wouldn't want to shatter that dream but she had to find some way of making it come true.

After several days of wrestling with the problem – mainly in maths classes and during morning assembly – Jessamy came up with another of her bright ideas. It hit her quite suddenly, in bed at night. Wham, bang! It was brilliant! It was foolproof! The sheer stunning cleverness of it took even Jessamy by surprise. What a blessing she was a creative sort of person! It wasn't everyone who could keep coming up with ideas the way she did.

Now that she had a plan of campaign, she couldn't

wait to put it into action – and went racing off first thing next morning to do so.

'Can I run through my Rain Forest dance?' she asked Karen, at the end of their *barre* exercises.

It was all supposed to have been so easy! She was going to run through the Rain Forest dance until she came to the *pirouette* section, and then – hey presto! – she was going to throw herself off balance. What could possibly be simpler?

What could be simpler, as she quickly discovered, was *not* throwing herself off balance. It was really most annoying, when she had been over and over it in her mind and was quite determined to carry it through, to find that at the last minute her body automatically behaved just the way it always did, just as it had been trained to do, taking not the least bit of notice of the new and confusing commands that were being thrown at it and, as a result, executing two very nearly perfect *pirouettes*.

'Bother!' said Jessamy, coming to a standstill.

'What's the matter?' Karen looked at her in surprise.

'Those *pirouettes* were *gruesome*,' said Jessamy.

'No, they weren't! They were fine.'

'They weren't. They were *gruesome*.'

'They didn't look gruesome to me.'

'Well, they felt gruesome. Let me do them again.'

The second time round, although still reluctant, her body obeyed her: she wobbled and almost fell, and ended up facing in the wrong direction.

'There!' said Jessamy. 'I knew there was something wrong.' Nobly (because she was proud of her *pirouettes*), she said, 'I do find them difficult sometimes, don't you?'

'I – I haven't really mastered them yet.' Karen said it in a great rush, her cheeks burning.

'I *thought* I had,' said Jessamy. 'Honestly, when you get them right they're dead easy. Do you want to have a go and I'll show you how to do it? 'Cause I know perfectly well in *theory*.'

'All right.' Karen scrambled eagerly to her feet.

'See, what you have to do, you have to find a spot and fix your eyes on it – '

'I already do that,' said Karen, 'but I keep losing it!'

'That's because you're not moving your head fast enough. You've got to let your body start turning, then your head comes after, but quickly – like this. Look!'

Jessamy executed three beautiful *pirouettes*, one after another.

'Slowly!' begged Karen. 'Do it slowly!'

They were five minutes late for assembly (which meant two punctuality marks), but by the time they left the gym Karen had mastered her first *pirouette*.

'It feels wonderful!' she said.

'It is,' said Jessamy. 'When you've got it right, you can go on turning practically for ever!'

'I'm going to practise,' said Karen.

It was a temptation to say, 'What will Madame Olga think?' but Jessamy knew that she mustn't. For once in her life, she was trying hard to be tactful.

'Why were you and Karen late?' said Sheela, as they went back to their classroom after assembly. 'Were you doing things together?'

'We were rehearsing my Rain Forest dance.'

'Why? Is she going to do it with you?'

'She might,' said Jessamy. She hadn't altogether given up on the idea. After all, now Karen had mastered *pirouettes* there wasn't any reason why she shouldn't.

'I suppose you like being with her better than you like being with us,' said Susan.

'I don't!' said Jessamy. 'It's just that I can talk about dancing with her.'

'You'll become a ballet bore,' said Susan, 'if you're not careful.'

'That's right,' said Sheela. 'You've got to have outside interests.'

Jessamy thought of her mum and dad, and Saul. They didn't have any outside interests. Lots of dancers didn't; they didn't have the time. She tried explaining this to Susan and Sheela but predictably they just shook their heads.

'You'll get narrow-minded,' said Susan, 'you will.'

Perhaps she already was. It was true that at the moment she couldn't think of anything except the Spirit of the Rain Forest and how to help Karen. It was also true that when she wasn't thinking of those particular things she was thinking about how to improve her turnout or how to achieve the perfect *arabesque* or whether she would ever make as brilliant a Lilac Fairy as Colleen McBride (currently one of her two favourite dancers at City Ballet, the other being Alessandro Corelli, who partnered her).

Did that make her narrow-minded? Susan would say yes, and Sheela would agree, and maybe they were right – but what could you do? If you were going to be a dancer it had to occupy your thoughts every waking moment. Dedication was what Jessamy's mum called it.

The next day was Saturday. Jessamy met Susan and Sheela in the shopping centre and mooched round for a bit, trying things on in the Clothes Mart (until an assistant came up and told them to stop it), reading the magazines in WH Smith, putting their money together to buy a beanburger and chips, of which Jessamy ate only a tiny portion for fear of getting fat. At home she was never allowed chips. Susan, shovelling them into her mouth as fast as she could go, said, 'You know what? You'll get anorexia if you're not careful.'

'No, I won't,' said Jessamy. 'I eat loads more than most people.'

Some of the kids at the Academy practically starved themselves, even at the age of eleven. Jessamy thought that was stupid, and so did Belinda Tarrant. She said, 'A bit of puppy fat never hurt anyone. If you look at pictures of Margot Fonteyn as a teenager she was quite moon-faced.' Jessamy wouldn't want to be moon-faced (even if it meant growing up as beautiful as Margot Fonteyn), but she certainly wasn't going to starve herself – she enjoyed her food too much. It was just that chips were definitely unhealthy.

'Yum, yum,' said Sheela, licking her lips. The maddening thing about Sheela was that she remained skinny as a rake in spite of stuffing herself with chips and crisps and chocolate. *And* having practically no exercise.

At midday Jessamy went home for lunch. It was Elke's weekend off and she had asked Jessamy to be punctual. She stayed just long enough to watch Jessamy

74

eat and then set off in her best up-to-date gear (a big black cloak and hat bought from the Clothes Mart) to meet what *she* said was a girlfriend. Jessamy didn't believe a word of it.

'It's a boyfriend really, isn't it?' she said.

'You M.Y.O.B.,' said Elke, tapping a finger to her nose. 'And no mischief, please! You behave until your dad comes. If any problem, you call your mother.'

Mum was at the studio, as usual; Dad was due back home that afternoon. He probably wouldn't want to get the car out because he would probably be jet-lagged and fit for nothing but going to bed, so Jessamy thought she had better telephone Karen and tell her to come by bus. Not having an over-conscientious Elke to fuss over her, Karen was quite used to jumping on buses and tubes by herself.

It was Karen's gran who answered the phone.

'Is that Jessamy?' she said. 'I'm so glad you've rung! I've been wanting to ring you, but I couldn't find your number. I'm getting a little worried about Karen. She hasn't come home yet. What time did she leave you?'

Jessamy, thrown, said, 'Um – oh! Ah – '

What fibs had Karen been telling now?

'She's never back later than twelve,' said her gran. 'Did she not meet you in the library the same as usual?'

'Um – n–no,' said Jessamy. 'We didn't actually – um – see each other.'

'So where can she have gone?' There was a note almost of panic in the old lady's voice. 'I said to her, lunch at twelve. It's nearly one o'clock!'

'I expect she'll be home soon,' said Jessamy. Karen had obviously gone to the Noran School to put herself

75

through class and had forgotten the time. Too busy practising her *pirouettes*, probably, 'I don't think anything will have happened to her,' said Jessamy, trying to sound comforting and grown-up.

'I do hope not,' said Karen's gran. 'While you're on the phone, my dear, I wonder if I might make a note of your number? Just in case.'

Quarter of an hour later, the telephone rang. Jessamy thought it was probably her dad, calling from the airport, but it was Karen's gran again.

'Oh, Jessamy,' she said, 'I'm so sorry to pester you like this, but that naughty girl still isn't back. I wonder . . . you don't have any idea where she might have gone, do you?'

Jessamy thought quickly. It was bad of Karen to upset her gran, but a secret was a secret and it wasn't up to Jessamy to give it away.

'She might be with – with one of our friends from school that isn't on the telephone, but lives quite near,' she said. 'Would you like me to go and see?'

'Oh, my dear, could you? If it's not putting you to too much trouble. The friend doesn't live too far away, does she?'

'No, not very,' said Jessamy. 'I can easily go round there. I'll tell her to come straight home.'

'And you'll ring me if she's not there?'

'I'm sure she will be,' said Jessamy.

She knew what it was like when you became obsessed with going over and over one particular step until you got it right. Time simply stood still. She wondered whether to take the bus down Fairhall Road or whether this could be counted as an emergency. She decided that it could – for after all, Karen's gran was old and might have a heart attack if she went on worrying for too long – and that it justified booking a cab through the cab company which her mum always used. Belinda Tarrant went everywhere by cab. She said that not having to drive oneself was one of life's little luxuries. Actually it was rather an expensive little luxury, but Jessamy reckoned her mum wouldn't mind one extra journey being added to her account. Going by bus would take for ever.

'Could you wait for me, please?' said Jessamy, in her best grown-up voice as the cab came to a halt outside the Noran School. 'I won't be a minute.'

'Right you are,' said the cabby. He knew Jessamy quite well; he had often taken her to places when Elke was sick or on holiday.

Jessamy pushed open the side gate and trod carefully down the passage to the back of the house. She couldn't hear any music so maybe Karen had already left – which would be all right, because it would mean she was on her way home.

Jessamy peered through one of the windows into the studio. At first she thought no one was in there, but then she looked again and what had seemed to be a shadow transformed itself into Karen, crouched on the floor at the back, clutching her ankle. Jessamy didn't hesitate: she threw open the double doors and bounded in.

'Karen! What's happened? What have you done?'

Karen's head came up. Her eyes, wide and startled, met Jessamy's.

'Have you hurt yourself?'

'I was – practising *pirouettes* and my – my foot went through the – the floorboards. I think I've d–done something to my ankle!'

'Let's have a look.' With cool professionalism, Jessamy dropped to her knees and took Karen's ankle between her hands. She knew about ankle injuries.

'Does it hurt when I do this?' she said.

'N–no. N–not specially. Just when I t–try to p–put any w–weight on it!'

'It's probably only a sprain,' said Jessamy. 'I don't think you've broken it.'

'It won't stop me dancing, will it?'

'Heavens, no!' said Jessamy. 'Well, only for a day or two. Not permanently. Listen, I rang your gran and she said you weren't home and she's dead worried 'cause she thought you were with me – ' two spots of colour appeared in Karen's cheeks – 'so I said I thought you might be with someone from school and I'd go and have a look.'

'How did you know?' whispered Karen.

'Can't tell you now – I've got a cab outside. I think you ought to go back to your gran before she thinks you've been kidnapped or something.'

'Yes.' Karen hobbled gingerly to her feet. 'I d–didn't mean to stay here for so long but I – I forgot the time and then – then the floorboards gave way and – '

'They're rotten,' said Jessamy. 'You're lucky it wasn't worse. Here!' She ran across and gathered up Karen's clothes. 'You'd better put these on. Your gran might think it odd if you turn up in a leotard.'

'You won't tell her, will you?'

'Not if you don't want me to.'

'It would upset her,' said Karen. 'She already feels bad about not having enough money to let me have proper ballet lessons.'

'She would have if it weren't for the book learning,' said Jessamy.

'I know; if she didn't have to pay for me to go to Coombe Hurst. But she thinks that's what Granddad wanted. She says it's what he left the money for and she c –' Karen stopped. 'How did you know about the book learning?' she said.

'Tell you later. Can you walk all right, or do you want to lean on me?'

'I expect I can hop,' said Karen.

The cab driver didn't actually pass any comment about Jessamy appearing from a derelict house with Karen hopping on one foot behind her, though he probably wondered.

'What are you going to say to your gran?' said Jessamy.

Karen looked at her, stricken. 'I don't know!'

'You could always say you went round to see Sheela and forgot what the time was, and then I came and said your gran was worried, and you went tearing out in such a rush you tripped over and did your ankle in.' Jessamy was an expert in such matters. When you had someone like Elke clucking round after you you occasionally had to resort to making things up.

'Couldn't I have gone to see Portia?' said Karen. 'I really did go to see her once. It wouldn't seem such a terrible fib.'

'Yes, but I said whoever it was wasn't on the telephone.'

'Isn't Sheela on the telephone?'

'She is at the shop but not at home 'cause they've only just moved and they're waiting for one to be put in.'

'Oh.' Karen heaved a sigh. 'All right,' she said. 'I'll say I went to Sheela's.'

'*I* don't know why you don't tell her the truth,' said Jessamy. 'I bet if she knew how desperate you were she'd let you leave Coombe Hurst and have ballet lessons instead.'

'Yes, but – ' tears sprang to Karen's eyes ' – then she'd feel she was letting Granddad down! He worked ever so hard to get enough money for me to have an education and then he died before he could see it happen. Gran wouldn't ever forgive herself if she spent the money on dancing classes.'

'But it's not fair on you!' cried Jessamy.

'I know, but the other way wouldn't be f–fair on G–Gran!'

Jessamy was silent a while.

'Sometimes you have to be ruthless to get anywhere in life,' she said.

Karen hiccuped and pulled a strand of damp hair away from her cheek.

'That's the trouble . . . I don't think I am very ruthless.'

I am, thought Jessamy; but Jessamy didn't need to be. Jessamy had all the advantages that an aspiring ballet dancer could possibly want.

She would just have to be ruthless enough for the two of them.

6

'It wasn't that I was spying on you,' said Jessamy. 'I mean – '

She stopped. What else could you call it but spying? She *had* been spying; creeping round after Karen, trying to find out where she went. Jessamy felt her cheeks fire up. She turned away: she wasn't used to embarrassing herself.

'It's all right,' said Karen. She pulled out her handkerchief. 'I expect I shouldn't have t–told all those l–lies!'

It was the following morning. Karen and Jessamy were sitting on the bed in Karen's bedroom, the walls of which were entirely covered in photographs of dancers, including several of Saul. There was Saul as Albrecht, Saul as Prince Siegfried, Saul in *Les Sylphides*, Saul as himself, looking rather sleek and glamorous. Even Jessamy, who had seen him unshaven in his pyjamas with his eyes still glued together in the early morning, could understand how it was that some girls just went to pieces over him. When he wanted to, Saul could look quite devastating.

Jessamy heaved a sigh. 'They weren't exactly *lies*,' she said.

'Yes, they were! They were lies!' Karen mopped despairingly at her eyes with a damp patch of handkerchief.

She was still inclined to be a bit weepy, not over her ankle, now swathed in a crepe bandage – the doctor had said it was only a very minor sprain – but over the loss of Madame Olga, for how could she go on pretending, even to herself? And how could she go back to the Noran School, after what had happened?

'I don't know what I'm going to do!' wept Karen.

'There's still the gym,' said Jessamy.

'It's not enough!' Karen blotted again at her eyes. 'I'll *have* to go back. I just won't dance on the rotten floorboards.'

Jessamy looked at her, frowning.

'I don't think you ought,' she said. 'I don't think it's safe.'

'It is if I just keep to one side of the room.'

'But what are you going to do when it's dark?' said Jessamy. 'You won't be able to see!'

'I'll take some candles.'

'Yes, and then you'll go and knock them over and set light to yourself!'

'No, I won't.' Karen sat up, straight-backed and cross-legged, on the bed. 'I'm not clumsy.'

'But suppose you were practising *pirouettes* and forgot they were there?'

'I'll put them on the windowsill.'

There didn't seem to be any argument to that. Jessamy sat, brooding, by Karen's side. She was already discovering Karen's apparent docility was deceptive. She might *seem* meek and mild, but she didn't let anyone, not even Jessamy, push her around. It was true she wasn't ruthless, but still she had Mum's famous 'rod of steel' going up her back. Mum always said that you couldn't get anywhere without a rod of steel.

'If your gran knew what you were doing,' said Jessamy, 'she'd be dead worried.'

The tears came welling back into Karen's eyes. Her gran was a sure way of getting to her. 'That's why I c—can't tell her!'

'I bet if you did she'd say it was dangerous – 'cause it *is* dangerous.' Even Jessamy could see that. 'You could get *murdered*.'

Karen stared at her, wide-eyed. 'How could I get murdered?'

'All by yourself in the dark, in an empty house. It's almost as bad as getting into a car with a strange man.'

'But what else can I do?' cried Karen.

'I don't know,' said Jessamy. 'I'm thinking about it. If you really won't tell your gran – '

'No! I can't! It would upset her.'

'But it's your whole future that's at stake,' urged Jessamy.

'I know.' Karen twisted her damp handkerchief round a finger.

'It's not as if it's just some passing phase.'

Passing phase was what some of Mum's pupils at the Academy suffered from. One minute they thought they wanted to be dancers and went rushing out to buy all the gear, the pink tights and the satin shoes and the shiny lycra leotards; the next it was too much like hard work and they couldn't be bothered any more.

'This is *serious*,' said Jessamy.

'I know, but – Gran loved Granddad s—so much and he k—killed himself making enough m—money for me to have an educ–cation! Gran would break her heart if I didn't have one.'

Karen's handkerchief was beyond redemption. Silently, Jessamy handed her a paper tissue from a box on the bedside table.

'She cried for months and m–months after Granddad died. Sending me to C–Coombe Hurst is the only thing that makes her happy 'cause she thinks it's what he w–wanted!'

'But she doesn't actually *know*.'

'Well, she d–does 'cause he used to talk of me going to university and that's something I'll n–never be c–clever enough to do!'

'Which is all right, 'cause you don't want to.'

'But he wanted me to!' Karen's tears burst out afresh. 'Sometimes I feel so g–guilty, telling Gran I'm s–studying when all I'm doing is p–practising ballet!'

Jessamy fell silent. She wondered how it must feel to love someone as deeply as Karen obviously loved her gran. Jessamy loved her mum and dad, of course, but it would never have occurred to her to consider their feelings above her own. Maybe it was because they weren't always there, as Karen's gran was. She was used to being without them for quite long stretches and to being able – more or less – to do whatever she wanted. She certainly didn't feel any pangs of conscience, or sense of responsibility towards them. Mum and Dad could take care of themselves.

She could see that it might be different for Karen with her gran. After all, Karen's gran hadn't *had* to look after Karen. Parents didn't have any choice. If they had a baby it was up to them to take care of it (as Jack would very soon discover. Jessamy bet *she* wouldn't be so happy when she had to keep changing nappies and getting covered in sick. Babies were always being sick. Nasty messy things). Karen's gran could quite easily, probably, have sent Karen to a children's home.

'I suppose you don't have any rich aunts and uncles?' said Jessamy.

Karen shook her head. 'Haven't got any aunts and uncles.'

'Oh, that's a pity. You could have asked them if they'd pay for your lessons. I mean, it would be an investment. One day when you're famous – '

'I'll never be famous at th–this rate!'

'You will,' said Jessamy. 'You've got to be! If I'm going to be, then so are you. You can't deny talent. There's got to be *some* way.'

'There isn't. Not if I haven't got anywhere to p–practise!'

'The thing is,' said Jessamy, 'even if you had you couldn't just go on teaching yourself.'

'I know!' Karen wept afresh. 'I couldn't even manage *p–pirouettes* until you sh–showed me!'

'This is it,' said Jessamy. 'You can't learn everything from books. You've done really well so far. I really thought there was a Madame Olga' (Karen blushed), 'but the more advanced you become the more difficult it gets. You really do need someone to help you.'

'There isn't anyone!'

'There's me,' said Jessamy.

Karen's tears stopped abruptly.

'You mean – y–you could teach me?'

85

'I could try,' said Jessamy. 'I taught you *pirouettes* OK.'

'But I haven't any m–money to p–pay you with!'

'I don't *want* paying.' Jessamy said it fiercely. 'I'd do it because you're my friend – and because you've got talent and it's a crime to waste talent. I wouldn't do it,' said Jessamy, 'if I didn't think it was worth it. It'll be fun – it'll be a challenge! But you'll have to do everything I say, like you would with a real teacher.'

'Oh, I will!' Karen nodded, earnestly. 'I'll work really hard, I promise you!'

'And you won't go back to that place any more? 'Cause I honestly don't think you should,' said Jessamy.

'Couldn't I just on a Saturday morning?' Karen said it pleadingly, almost as if, from now on, she had to ask Jessamy's permission before she could do anything at all.

'Maybe just on Saturday mornings,' agreed Jessamy, 'but not after school!'

'All right.' Karen gave her eyes one final blot with her paper handkerchief. 'And we'll meet in the gym same as usual.'

'Seven-thirty sharp,' said Jessamy. 'Then we can put in a full hour.'

Much though she enjoyed teaching Karen all that she herself had been taught – she enjoyed the sense of achievement when Karen finally mastered a new and difficult step; she also enjoyed the sense of power, of being able to say 'Do this. Do that' and of seeing that they were done – still Jessamy was aware that it was not the final answer. Sooner or later, and probably quite soon, Karen was going to need a proper teacher.

Half term was coming up, and Jessamy, ever resourceful, had another of her ideas. A good one, this time. This one was bound to work!

At half term, even the Academy closed for a few days. That meant that Mum would be at home.

'When you come over tomorrow,' said Jessamy, as she and Karen left the gym on Friday morning, 'why don't you bring your practice clothes and we could do a bit more work on your *battements fondus*.'

Karen looked at her, worried.

'Are they very bad?'

'They're not *bad*,' said Jessamy (feeling a bit mean, since in fact Karen had perfectly respectable *battements fondus*. But it was all in a good cause). 'It's just that they could do with a bit more practice. So could mine, as a matter of fact. We could work on them together.'

'All right,' said Karen. She sounded happier now that she knew Jessamy had problems as well.

It was a pity they couldn't do centre work, which was what Karen really needed to practise, but either Mum or Dad was bound to be in the sitting-room and even if they weren't Karen would probably be too bashful to do anything where she ran the risk of being seen. Jessamy's bedroom wasn't enormous, but at least it was big enough for some simple *barre* work, *and* she had a proper portable *barre*.

'Are you going to be here at tea time?' Jessamy asked her Mum, on Saturday morning.

'Yes, I expect so,' said Belinda Tarrant. 'Why?'

'Karen's coming. She'd be ever so thrilled if she could meet you. Dad too, of course.'

Belinda Tarrant rolled her eyes.

'We are not exhibits in a zoo,' she said.

'It's the price you pay for being famous,' retorted Jessamy.

'Famous we are not. Famous we never were. Just slightly well known.'

'It's still the price you pay. *I* wouldn't complain,' said Jessamy, 'if I were dancing leading roles and people wanted to see me.'

'My dear Jessamy, I haven't danced leading roles for over a decade. I'm nothing but a humble ballet teacher.'

'*Humble*?' said Jessamy. 'Huh!'

'Oh, get away!' Belinda Tarrant flicked at her with a scarf she was holding. 'Horrible child! In my day we never spoke to our parents like that.'

Cleverly – or so she thought – Jessamy engineered it so that she and Karen were still practising their *battements fondus* when Elke called up the stairs that tea was ready.

'We'll have to go down as we are,' said Jessamy.

'Like this?' Karen sounded doubtful. 'Won't anyone mind?'

'This is a *ballet* family,' Jessamy reminded her. 'They're used to it. Come on!'

Karen, obviously still not quite comfortable with the idea, pattered down the stairs after Jessamy. Everyone was in the basement – Mum, Dad, Elke, even Jacquetta and the Bottler, who were staying for a couple of days. Good. That was good. That was what she had hoped for. Jessamy held open the door for Karen and watched approvingly as she walked through. In her leotard and tights, with her hair pulled back into a regulation bun, Karen looked every inch a dancer. Jessamy felt proud of herself. Surely the family couldn't fail to notice?

She had underestimated them: Jessamy's family could be blind as bats to anything which did not directly concern themselves. Mum glanced up and said, 'Oh, hallo. You're Katie, are you? Sit down and have some tea.' Dad said, 'Jessamy, have you seen my *Beaumont on Ballet*? I can't seem to find it anywhere.' Jacquetta didn't even bother to look up. The Bottler was the only one who showed any signs of appreciation.

'What have we here?' he said. 'Another aspiring Fonteyn?'

Karen blushed. Jessamy said, 'This is Karen. Karen – ' she said it loudly, for her mum's benefit ' – this is my sister Jacquetta, and this is her husband, Neville.'

Someone in the family had to show some manners.

Dad said, 'Hallo, there, Karen. Now, look, Jessamy, about my *Beaumont* – '

'I haven't seen it,' said Jessamy. Why should she want his rotten *Beaumont*?

'Are you still doing your tacky little end-of-term number?' said Jacquetta.

'It's not tacky,' said Jessamy. 'It's all about rain forests and the environment.'

'Oh, how very earnest!'

'It's good,' said Karen.

Jessamy beamed at her, gratefully. Jacquetta said, 'Yes, I'm sure, but it's so *tacky*.'

'Jack gave up ballet to have babies,' said Jessamy, investing the word with as much scorn as she could muster.

'Only one,' said Jacquetta.

'For the moment,' added the Bottler.

Dad stretched out greedily for a hunk of cake. 'If someone's gone and removed my *Beaumont* without telling me I'll poxy well flay them!'

'Wasn't me,' said Jessamy.

'It better hadn't be!'

'It wasn't.'

'Karen, have some scone,' said Elke. 'Scone with clotted cream and home-made jam. It's very good.'

'She can't have clotted cream – ' Jessamy said it angrily: you'd have thought Elke would have known, by now ' – she's a dancer!'

'She look to me like she's too thin,' said Elke.

'Dancers are thin. They're supposed to be thin.'

Elke made an impatient scoffing sound in the back of her throat: she had no sympathy with what she called 'food fads'. No one else took the slightest bit of notice. Dad piled a plate with cake and scones and carried it off to another part of the house with a cup of tea the colour of black mud, the way he liked it. The Bottler leafed through Elke's copy of *Elle* magazine. Mum sat and talked to Jacquetta about babies. She didn't even *like* babies. Jessamy felt quite sick with the lot of them.

Afterwards, back in her bedroom, she said, 'I really have to apologise for my family. They have manners like wart hogs. Dad was really *gross.*'

'He was cross,' said Karen, ''cause of his book.'

'Stupid book! I haven't touched it.'

At six o'clock they went downstairs to find Elke, to take Karen home in the car. As they walked round to the garage, they bumped into Saul on his way in.

'You again!' said Jessamy. 'What is it this time? Strained your big toe?'

'I am not on tonight, *ducky.*' Saul twiddled a finger in her hair. 'It's your beloved in *Swan Lake.*'

'Sandro?' She had seen him in *Swan Lake* loads of times. 'So when are you on again?'

'Monday, Tuesday, Wednesday matinée ... that enough for you? Am I earning my keep?'

'What are you dancing on Wednesday?' asked Jessamy.

'*Spectre* and *Petrushka.* Why?'

Jessamy had yet another of her ideas.

'Could you get us tickets?'

'I daresay I might. If you asked nicely.'

Jessamy spun round to Karen, hiding scarlet-faced behind her.

'Shall we go and see him?'

Karen seemed too overawed to speak. She opened her mouth, but no sound came out.

'If you could very sweetly and kindly get tickets for us,' said Jessamy, 'we should like to come on Wednesday, please.'

'In that case – ' Saul turned and saluted them as he sprang up the steps to the front door ' – I shall pull out all the stops!'

When Jessamy arrived home after delivering Karen to her door, she confronted her mum in the sitting-room.

'Don't you think that Karen is the perfect shape for a dancer?'

'Is she? I didn't really notice.'

'Well, she is.'

'Good. That's nice for her.'

'It's not nice,' said Jessamy, ''cause she can't afford ballet lessons.'

'So what am I supposed to do about it? I'm not a charity institution. Honestly, you're like one of those awful ballet mothers, thrusting their puddinglike offspring at me!'

'Karen is not puddinglike!' yelled Jessamy.

There were times when her family really were the *pits*.

7

'Go by yourself?' said Elke. 'To the *theatre*?'

'I've been lots of times by myself,' boasted Jessamy.

'This I do not believe!'

'I have, honestly! You ask Mum.'

It was true that Jessamy had sometimes *sat* by herself, while her mum or dad, or both of them, had wandered off backstage to talk to people; not quite true that she had ever actually gone there by herself. But it was easy enough! Jessamy knew the way. You took a tube from Chiswick Park to the Temple, and then you walked up Arundel Street to the Strand, turned right towards Fleet Street, and there it was, the Fountain Theatre. She had only once gone there by public transport, and that was with Saul, but she could remember it just as clearly as if it had been a sequence of ballet steps.

'I do not like,' said Elke. 'London is bad place for a young girl.'

It was really very tiresome, never being allowed to go anywhere by yourself.

'I never have any fun at all,' grumbled Jessamy.

'Fun? You think you don't have fun? I will tell you, young lady, you are most privileged person! Spoilt is what you are, if you ask me. One big sulk because she is not allowed to go on the gallivant!'

'I don't want to go on the gallivant! I just want to go to the theatre!'

'So go! I come with you.'

'*You*?' said Jessamy.

Elke coming with them was the last thing she wanted. She had pictured it being just her and Karen, all cosy together, going up to the bar in the interval to beg lemonade and biscuits from old Mrs P., discussing the performances, visiting Saul backstage afterwards. They didn't want Elke tagging along!

'Hah! See how that takes the wind from out of her sails,' said Elke.

'Well, but you don't even like ballet,' pouted Jessamy.

'So I make sacrifice for you. Like I say, you are spoilt child.'

'But I don't w – '

'Is part of my job,' said Elke. 'Is what I am paid for. And besides -- ' did a slight pinkish tinge creep into her cheek or was Jessamy only imagining it? ' – maybe I see your brother dance, maybe I change my mind.'

Oh! So that was it! Someone else who had a thing about Saul. *Bother*. That would mean they wouldn't only be stuck with Elke sitting there with them, and shepherding them about during the interval, she would also want to come cramming backstage with them afterwards.

She complained bitterly to Karen, when she went round to visit her.

'It's such a *drag*. She only let me come by myself today 'cause it's the middle of the morning.'

'Mm. They get worried. But I suppose eleven is quite young still.'

'Not as young as all that. Some p – '

'Listen! I've got something to show you.' Karen snatched at her hand. 'Come and see what I've done!'

She went scampering off up the stairs with Jessamy in tow. Karen plainly didn't care that they were going to be stuck with boring Elke.

'Look!' She threw open the door of her bedroom. The bed had gone, and most of the furniture. 'I asked Gran if I could move into the spare room and use this for practice, and she said yes, if I really wanted, so long as I didn't thump about and bring the ceiling down, so I moved everything out, as much as I could – everything except the wardrobe.' Karen giggled, excitedly. 'Gran thinks I'm mad! The spare room's so tiny I haven't got room to breathe, hardly. But what's it matter, if I'm only sleeping there? I'm going to try and find a long mirror in a second-hand shop, then all I'll need is a *barre*. What I'd really like is one like you've got. Do you think they're very expensive?'

'Haven't the faintest,' said Jessamy.

She knew she ought to be showing more enthusiasm, but she was still smarting from Elke saying she was spoilt. How could she be spoilt when Elke did nothing but nag at her and her dad was hardly ever there and her mum was too busy even to talk to her? Far from being spoilt, she was *deprived*. She wouldn't have minded so much if it were Mum or Dad coming to the ballet with them. In fact, it would be quite good if Mum or Dad were coming because then perhaps they would be forced to take notice of Karen. But of course Dad was going off again, to Frankfurt this time, and Mum was talking at a conference in Edinburgh, which meant staying overnight, leaving Elke in charge, so that now they were stuck with her whether they liked it or not. It was just absolutely *pathetic* that people of nearly twelve couldn't be trusted to go to the theatre by themselves.

'. . . every afternoon when I come home from school.'

Karen was still burbling on about her new studio. Jessamy gazed round, ungraciously.

'It's not big enough to do centre work.'

'Oh, well, no, of course! But I can do that in the gym.'

'What about school holidays?' said Jessamy. 'You won't be able to use the gym then.'

It was almost as if she had taken out a pin and physically burst the bubble of Karen's excitement. Karen's face fell. The light went out of her eyes.

'No, I know,' she said.

'And you won't be able to go back to the Noran School much longer, either,' said Jessamy. 'They're going to knock down all that block and put up a supermarket. I saw it in the paper.'

She didn't know why, all of a sudden, she felt the need to be mean. Just because Elke had had a go at her, she didn't have to have a go at Karen. Karen hadn't done anything to deserve it. It was just that it was so . . . so *idiotic*, imagining that you could ever learn ballet on your own, in your bedroom. If it were that easy, everyone would be doing it.

'When are they going to pull it down?' whispered Karen.

'Oh! I don't know. It didn't say. Probably not for ages.'

'I thought maybe, in the holidays, it would be all right if I went there – '

But what was the *point*? The gym, the studio, her bedroom . . . Jessamy felt a moment of angry irritation. It was just playing at being a dancer! It was nothing but make-believe. If Karen had any real backbone she would go to her gran and tell her, straight out, 'I don't *want* to go to Coombe Hurst! I want to go to ballet school.' So what if her gran were upset? Sometimes it was necessary to upset people. You didn't want to, but it couldn't be helped; it was either them or you. If you let yourself be trampled on, you'd never get anywhere – specially not as a dancer. The world of ballet might look deliciously frothy and foamy, but Jessamy knew, from growing up with dancers, that those who inhabited it all had Belinda Tarrant's rod of steel going up their backs.

'You're too soft,' said Jessamy, 'that's your trouble. Just because you don't want to hurt your gran . . . you'll never make it if you're not prepared to tread on a few toes. You'll just be wasting your time. *And* your talent. And that's even worse. Wasting talent is a crime.'

Karen looked at her, stricken.

'Don't you think I'm making any progress?'

'Why ask me? I'm not a teacher! You need to go to a proper school. You can't carry on like this – ' Jessamy waved an impatient hand round the empty bedroom. 'I mean . . . what do you think you're going to *do*?'

Karen, crestfallen, hung her head.

'I'd thought – perhaps – if you could go on teaching me until they let me leave school, then maybe – maybe I could get a – a scholarship, or . . . something.'

'That's just crazy talk!' Jessamy said it witheringly. 'It's *years* before you can leave school. And I'll be gone by then. I'm going to Central when I'm thirteen. I can't go on teaching you. You'd have to go back to doing it by yourself and by the time you left school it'd be far too late. Anyway, knowing your gran, she'd want you to stay on into the sixth and try for A levels, and then she'd want you to try for university, and – '

'I'll never get into university! I'm not clever enough.'

'So all this isn't just a waste of talent, it's a waste of your granddad's money, as well! It'd be far better if it was spent on teaching you something you're good at. Because you *are* good.'

Jessamy's rage had burnt itself out. She felt ashamed, now. When she had arrived Karen had been happy and excited, eager to show off her lovely new studio. In just five short minutes Jessamy had managed to ruin all her pleasure and totally undermine her confidence into the bargain. Perhaps Elke was right and she *was* spoilt.

'Oh, look! Don't worry,' she said. 'We're bound to think of something.' Jessamy would think of something. It was the least she could do. 'Let's try out your new studio!'

'I haven't got a *barre*,' muttered Karen.

'Has your gran got a towel thing in her bathroom? One of those stand things you drape them over? We could use that!'

Jessamy went racing off down the passage to return triumphantly dragging the towel rack behind her.

'There! You can stand one side, I'll stand the other. It's amazing what you can do,' said Jessamy, 'if you just put your mind to it.'

The next day was Wednesday, when they were going up to town. Elke was nervous of driving in heavy traffic and she seemed to think it not right using Mum's cab service, so they collected Karen and all trailed down to Chiswick Park tube. Jessamy actually didn't mind going by tube – it made it seem more of an outing. It also made her feel pleasantly important, as Elke didn't know the way from the Temple underground to the theatre and Jessamy did. Jessamy also, of course, knew most of the front-of-house staff – the ladies in the box office, the programme sellers, Jim the fireman and Mr Waldron, the front-of-house manager. They all waved at her or came over to say hallo.

Because it was a matinée and out of the tourist season, Saul had been able to get them seats in the circle.

'This is good,' said Jessamy, settling herself down. 'I like being in the circle – you can see better from here. Stalls are horrible. There's always some great tall person in your way, and anyhow you can't see the patterns properly.'

'What patterns?' said Elke.

'Patterns on stage. Made by the dancers.' She hoped Elke wasn't going to show them up by asking silly questions. Jessamy half turned in her seat towards Karen. 'This is my very favourite theatre,' she said.

The Royal Opera House might be grander, but Jessamy had grown up with the Fountain. She loved its faded splendour – the beaming cherubs frolicking about the ceiling (some had lost their arms or legs or noses), the glittering chandelier precariously hanging overhead, the blue and gold, slightly tarnished, of the boxes (where she sometimes sat with Mum and Dad), the musty smell of the old seats. Best of all she loved the blue and gold curtain, with its loops and its tassels, rolling majestically upwards at the start of a performance, billowing down again at the end. Jack, predictably, said it was 'tacky . . . place needs a facelift', but Jessamy loved it just as it was.

'So what are these ballets that we are to see?' said Elke.

'*Spectre de la Rose, Petrushka* and *Children's Games*. It tells you all about them in the programme.'

'I've always wanted to see *Spectre de la Rose*,' said Karen.

'It's one of my favourites,' nodded Jessamy. 'Jack says it's yucky, but I don't think it is.'

The curtain went up on *Children's Games*, a slight piece by Lloyd Parsons, one of the boys in the company. It was fun, though nothing very much more.

'Mum says it's just intended as a *bonne bouche*,' said Jessamy, applauding along with everyone else.

'*Bonne bouche*!' Elke clicked her tongue, disapprovingly. In spite of sometimes using German phrases when her English ran out (though that didn't happen very often), Elke held that it was nothing but affectation, not to mention downright bad manners, to sprinkle your conversation with foreign phrases. 'You have no English word for this?'

'Titbit?' said Jessamy.

'Titbit. So why not say so? Why always in French?'

'Well, because lots of ballet terms *are* in French.'

Elke sniffed. Jessamy sometimes had the feeling that Elke held the ballet and everything to do with it in total contempt, which was odd considering she worked for a ballet family. Maybe after she had seen Saul she would change her opinions.

'I hope she doesn't make fun,' whispered Jessamy, in Karen's ear.

'Make fun?' Karen looked at her, wide-eyed. 'What of?'

Jessamy nodded towards the stage, as the curtain rose on *Le Spectre*. Gemma Dugard was dancing the young girl who comes home after the ball and falls asleep, still in her ball gown, and dreams. Gemma was young and beautiful: just right for the part. Saul was dancing the spirit of the rose which she had worn at her breast that night.

On Jessamy's birthday last year she had invited Susan and Sheela to an evening performance of *Spectre* – *Spectre*, *Sylphides* and Act II of *Swan Lake*. They had all sat in a box with Belinda Tarrant. Susan and Sheela had spent the evening passing Mum's opera glasses to and fro between them, making personal remarks about the dancers – 'Ugh! She's ever so ugly!' 'Heavens, look at his *make-up*!' It had been a mistake to bring them; but the biggest mistake of all had been to bring them to *Spectre*. The sight of a man – even one as handsome as Saul – dressed up in pink petals pretending to be a rose had been too much for them.

'He looks as if he's got a bath cap on his head!'

'Is he *naked*? Apart from the petals?'

'He is! He's naked!'

He wasn't, of course, but that didn't stop the two of them goggling and giggling and snatching at the opera glasses. Mum had said afterwards, 'It's the last time I take any of *your* friends to the ballet. Little philistines!'

Karen didn't giggle. She sat forward, enthralled, on the edge of her seat. Elke didn't giggle either, which perhaps wasn't surprising since Elke was not really a giggly sort of person, but Jessamy had braced herself for the odd derisive snort. She could understand that a ballet with a man dancing a rose, with pink petals all over him, might not perhaps be the best introduction for a person who wasn't sympathetic, but, after all, she hadn't planned on bringing Elke. If she had planned it then she would have picked something a bit more butch and obviously masculine – *Le Corsaire*, for example, or *Prince Igor*.

'That was *wonderful*,' breathed Karen, as they made their way up to the bar during the interval.

Elke looked at her. She seemed amused.

'I think maybe the costume is not help.'

'That costume,' said Jessamy, angrily, 'is a copy of the original.'

'So, but fashions change.'

'Not in ballet.'

That wasn't strictly true – today's ballerinas wouldn't be seen dead in some of the costumes worn by, say, Anna Pavlova or Adeline Genée. Too cluttered. Too frilly and fussy. But there were some ballets where the costumes were traditional, and *Spectre de la Rose* was one of them, so Elke could just go and – and drown herself! Jessamy turned rather huffily away.

'Maybe *Petrushka* is better,' said Elke.

Jessamy humped a shoulder.

'More of a story . . . what does your brother dance? He dance Petrushka?'

'No.' Look in your programme if you want to find out. *Daring* to criticise! Elke, who knew nothing about anything. The cheek of it!

'Saul's dancing the Moor,' said Karen.

Saul never danced Petrushka, probably because Dad had made his name in the role. Strictly speaking he wasn't really tall enough to dance the Moor, who ought to tower over poor lovelorn Petrushka, but it didn't matter since Petrushka was danced by Piet van den Berg, one of the shortest dancers in the company. Gemma Dugard was the Ballerina, pert and pretty with her rouged cheeks, running along on her points, with her doll's jerky movements, as she blew her toy trumpet. The Ballerina was one of the roles which Jessamy longed to dance: already she knew it by heart. If only Mum would let her go on point!

Petrushka was a success even with the sceptical Elke. It could hardly be anything else, thought Jessamy, watching as the braggart Moor, in his bright silks and satins, chased Petrushka round the stage, scimitar in hand. The Ballerina teetered after them, a fixed smile on her lips, still blowing her trumpet. She was a flirt, thought Jessamy. An inflamer of passions. There was poor Petrushka desperately in love with her, and there was she flaunting herself in front of the Moor, even to the extent of sitting on his lap and having a cuddle with him. (Jessamy wondered if Saul enjoyed Gemma sitting on his lap and cuddling with him, or whether he just accepted it as part of the ballet. She thought probably he just accepted it. Mum had once said that ballet was 'really quite sexless in spite of all the bare flesh'.)

Of course the true villain of the piece was the heartless puppet master. He didn't believe that puppets had feelings and wouldn't have cared even if they had. He enjoyed setting the Moor and Petrushka against each other, just to entertain the crowds. He thought it amusing that Petrushka should lose his heart to the Ballerina. It was all part of the show when the jealous Moor finally caught up with Petrushka and slashed at him with his scimitar.

The people who were watching (the people in the ballet, that is) all gasped in horror. They thought that Petrushka was a real person – they thought he had been killed – but the puppet master contemptuously picked up the limp body and showed them: nothing but a sawdust doll! No need to shed any tears. Poor Petrushka!

It served the evil showman right when at the end of the ballet Petrushka's ghost suddenly appeared over the rooftops, amidst the swirling snowflakes. A sawdust doll come back to haunt him! Maybe in future, thought Jessamy, he would treat his puppets better.

Elke nodded judiciously as the applause broke out.

'This one I do not mind so much. Though it is a pity,' she added, 'that Saul had to paint his face. It could have been anyone dancing it.'

It could not, thought Jessamy, crossly; not if you knew Saul. Jessamy would recognise her brother from the way he moved even if he had his head tied up in a sack.

'Let's go back and see him,' she said.

Karen's face, predictably, turned tomato red.

'*Can* we?'

'Of course we can! I always do.'

'Won't he mind? It's all right for you, you're his sister, but – '

'You're a fan,' said Jessamy. 'Everyone needs their fans.'

'But they do not perhaps always want them crowding in their dressing room,' said Elke. 'I think it best maybe we go straight back.'

Jessamy looked at her, haughtily. She might have to do what Elke said at home, but here in the theatre Jessamy was in command. What did Elke know about anything? Why, she wouldn't even know where the pass door was!

'*I'*m going backstage,' she said, 'and so's Karen. You can wait for us outside.'

Elke pursed her lips. 'Jessamy, I really think your brother will not wish to be bothered at such a time.'

'Pooh!' said Jessamy, rudely. *Amateurs* – she couldn't stand them. She pushed past Elke, pulling Karen with her.

'See you outside!' she called, but of course Elke had to follow. When it came to it, she couldn't resist.

Because it was a matinée, there weren't too many people in Saul's dressing room.

'Hi!' Saul was busy wiping his face clean of black make-up. 'So you dragged Elke along as well, did you? How did she like it?'

'Very nice, thank you,' said Elke.

'Except that it was a pity you had to paint yourself

black,' said Jessamy, 'as it could have been anyone dancing.'

Saul grinned. 'I see! That puts me in my place, doesn't it?'

'No! Really!' protested Elke. (That would teach her, thought Jessamy. Saying Jessamy was spoilt.) 'Really, of course I am knowing it is you.'

'She knew in *Spectre*,' said Jessamy. 'Could hardly help knowing there, considering you had hardly any clothes on.'

Elke's face grew red as a ripe tomato. 'Jessamy!'

'What there was of it,' said Jessamy, 'your costume, I mean, she thinks is old-fashioned.'

'She's dead right,' said Saul, 'it is! I've been fighting a battle for years to have it junked.'

'But it's *traditional*,' said Jessamy, shocked. 'It's what Nijinsky wore!'

'So were a lot of other things that you'd be laughed off stage for if you appeared in them today. Either laughed off stage or arrested. How about you, K – ' He stopped. 'Katrina?'

'Karen!' snapped Jessamy.

'Karen. How did you like it?'

'I thought it was lovely,' said Karen.

'She didn't think the costume was old-fashioned,' said Jessamy, 'did you?'

Karen blushed, shaking her head.

'She probably did, but doesn't like to say so.'

'To me,' said Elke, 'this man is the *spirit* of the rose, not the rose itself. So my view, if this is the case, he should be a young girl's dream – '

'Not a ponce in a pink petal bath hat. Precisely.' Saul

106

nodded. 'I couldn't have put it better myself. Jess, chuck us that towel, will you? Ta.'

Because of Elke being there, Saul hardly spoke to Karen and Jessamy at all. He hardly even noticed Karen. It simply wasn't fair.

Jessamy telephoned him next day, at his flat in town that he shared with another dancer in the company. (Saul could quite easily have lived at home, but he said it 'cramped his style', whatever that was supposed to mean. Jessamy privately thought it meant that he was having love affairs, which wouldn't surprise her in the least.)

'Saul?' she said. 'You know my friend Karen?'

'Do I know your friend Karen? Oh, yes! Your friend Karen. The little blonde who likes the pink petal bath cap. What about her?'

At least he had noticed that she was blonde. Encouraged, Jessamy said, 'Did you think she looked like a dancer?'

'I don't think I thought anything at all. Should I have done?'

'Yes, because she *does* look like a dancer. She's really got talent, she's taught herself out of a book, but now she needs proper lessons and her gran can't afford them. Do you think – '

'What? The answer, I should warn you, is almost certainly no.'

'Do you think – ' Jessamy said it doggedly ' – that if you came and gave her a lesson – '

'*Me*?'

'So that you could see her dance and tell Mum she's a deserving case.'

107

'Oh, come off it, Jess! You know what the old girl'd say . . . "*I am not –* " ' Saul mimicked Belinda Tarrant's light, crisp tones to perfection ' " – *a charity institution.*" '

'But, Saul, Karen is really really good!'

'Yes, I'm sure,' said Saul. 'Just like Tracey and Donna and Sharon and my-little-darling-who-went-up-on-her-points-at-the-age-of-two. Forget it, kid! The world is full of 'em!'

The trouble with her family, thought Jessamy bitterly, was that they were all too *cynical*.

8

'Right! Across the diagonal, one at a time. Jessamy, will you lead the way, please?'

Jessamy, positioning herself for a *pirouette*, caught an exchange of glances between Selma Chadwick and Donna Fletcher. She knew what they were thinking: *favouritism*.

Just because Jessamy was Belinda Tarrant's daughter. Well, it wasn't true. Mum never showed favouritism; if anything, she tended to be harder on Jessamy than anyone else (though some might have said that that in itself was a form of favouritism. Better to be taken notice of, even if it did mean constant criticism, than to be ignored). But one thing Mum hardly ever did and that was put Jessamy at the front of the class or ask her to take the lead. She was only doing it now because Jessamy's *pirouettes* were indisputably the strongest. Oh, what bliss it would be when she could do them on point! How fast she would move! How she would spin and dazzle!

Jessamy reached the far corner of the room, taking care to end neatly, as she had started, in fourth position. She stood, leaning against the *barre*, watching as the rest of the class followed. Selma, with her fat thighs. Donna, off balance as usual. Wendy Adams all over the place. Dawn Collier travelling in the wrong direction.

There wasn't a single one of them likely to make the grade – well, no, perhaps that was a slight exaggeration. Jennifer Ellis and Lucy Skinner weren't too bad. If Jenny didn't grow too tall and Lucy could keep her weight under control they might stand a chance. *Just*. They were more likely to end up as teachers. They weren't anywhere near as good as Karen, either of them.

It wasn't fair! All these no-hopers with their wrong-shaped bodies and their lack of talent cluttering up the studios and people like Karen, people with *real* talent, condemned to struggle alone in their bedrooms. Selma's mum worked all week on the tills in Marks & Spencer, up in Oxford Street, just to pay for Selma's ballet classes (and much good they did her. With thighs like that. Like *tree* trunks). Why couldn't Karen's gran go out and work? She wasn't as old as all that.

She knew what Karen would say. Jessamy had hinted once before that maybe if Karen's gran got a job then she would be able to pay for Karen to have both ballet lessons *and* go to Coombe Hurst. Karen had been shocked.

'I couldn't ask Gran to do that! She gets these terrible pains in her knees, so bad she sometimes can't even walk. She couldn't go out scrubbing floors.'

Jessamy hadn't said anything about scrubbing floors. Surely there were other things that Karen's gran could do?

'But why should she?' had said Karen.

Why shouldn't she, was what Jessamy thought. She had chosen to bring Karen up. Surely it was her responsibility to make sure she had the opportunity to use

110

the talent God had given her? After all, it wasn't every-one who was blessed with talent. You only had to look at Mum's Tuesday class to see that. Even Jenny and Lucy were only a bit better than average; they were never going to be star material.

Belinda Tarrant never discussed her pupils in front of Jessamy, but Jessamy had once overheard her talking to Dad. She had said that 'apart from Jessamy, of course, and Marcia Eagling, there really isn't anyone I'd call promising'.

Marcia had won a place, last term, at the Arts Edu-cational in Tring. That only left Jessamy. Which did *not* make her big-headed, as some of the others tried to claim. Jessamy knew her strong points, but she also knew her weaknesses.

'*Line*, Jessamy! Focus your eyes – watch those shoulders. *Smoothly*, please! No jerking.'

Allegro was her forte: adage all too often her down-fall. Ignorant people tended to judge a dancer solely by the number of *pirouettes* and *fouettés* they could do, and the speed at which they did them. Those who knew, the true ballet enthusiasts, looked for something more. The line of an *arabesque*, the carriage of head and arms: balance and control and poetry. Jessamy knew she still had a long way to go.

'Don't stand there like a garden rake! Put some feeling into it!'

The others liked it when the great Jessamy Hart had her knuckles rapped. But when she did something well, like today's *pirouettes*, they put it down to favouritism: implying that if she had been anyone else she would have been roundly criticised along with the rest.

111

'All right for some,' muttered Donna, as they filed into the changing room at the end of class.

'Yes, it is, isn't it?' said Jessamy. Donna's dad was some big pot in industry. Donna not only learnt ballet, she also studied piano, owned her own pony and had a television set and a video in her bedroom. Even Jessamy didn't have that (in spite of Elke saying she was spoilt).

'What are you talking about?' said Selma.

'What she said.' Jessamy jerked her head in Donna's direction. 'It's all right for some.'

'Yes, and we know who,' muttered Donna.

Selma stripped her tights away from her horrible fat thighs. 'I bet we could all get noticed if we had the right parents.'

They were so jealous it was unbelievable. Karen wasn't jealous. If she had been, Jessamy wouldn't have bothered with her, no matter how much talent she had. She was sick of all the spite and backbiting; she'd had enough of it at ballet classes. What did they have to complain about, Donna and Selma, compared with Karen?

'Four classes a week,' said Selma. 'Some of us have to make do with only two.'

'Yes, and some people have to make do with none at all,' snapped Jessamy.

If Karen could have just one class a week, it would be something. Not enough, of course; but at least she would be able to show what she could do. How much did one class a week cost? Maybe if Jessamy took money out of her building society account . . . but Elke would never let her. She would go and tell Mum and Mum would tell Jessamy to stop being so silly.

'I am not a charity institution, and neither are my daughters! That money was put there for you. For your future. Not to go throwing away on pudding-faced nobodies.'

Mum had more than a rod of steel going up her back: Jessamy sometimes thought her heart was made of steel as well. Naturally she had to defend herself against all the dreadful pushy ballet mothers thrusting their offspring at her, Jessamy could quite understand that. She had seen enough of people's mothers to know that ballet teachers had to arm themselves against them. Selma's mother, for instance. She was a big solid woman with huge thighs, who simply didn't seem to realise that Selma was going to grow up just like her, and that thighs like giant oaks had no place on a ballet stage. She still kept buttonholing Mum and trying to get her to say that Selma was the greatest thing since Anna Pavlova.

She had to take pupils like Selma, if only because pupils like Karen were so rare. Marcia Eagling had been her last success: she was looking to Jessamy to be the next. So wouldn't you think, if talent were so scarce, she'd listen when Jessamy tried to tell her about Karen? It wasn't as if Jessamy were a ballet mother (though she was almost beginning to feel like one). She was *Belinda Tarrant's daughter*. Didn't that count for anything?

It seemed not, in spite of what her fellow pupils at the Academy chose to believe. Belinda Tarrant had heard too many tales of second Anna Pavlovas and of Margot-Fonteyns-in-the-making. It had made her cynical, so that now she wouldn't trust anyone or anything; only the evidence of her own eyes.

Shortly after half term Mrs Richmond asked Jessamy how her solo was coming along.

'Had any ideas yet?'

'Yes, it's all worked out,' said Jessamy. 'I've been practising it for weeks.'

'Oh, splendid! I knew we could rely on you. When shall we be able to see it? At the dress rehearsal? Or would you like to unveil it before? Perhaps you should come along next week – we're rehearsing on stage for the first time. Doing a full run through. Two o'clock Saturday. Could you manage that?'

'Yes, that would be all right,' said Jessamy.

'In the meantime, I'll get Mrs Markham to come and measure you up for a costume. You can tell her what sort of thing you had in mind.'

Karen was obviously disappointed, though she tried not to show it, when Jessamy explained that she wouldn't be able to see her on Saturday as usual.

'Why don't you come to the rehearsal?' said Jessamy.

'Oh, but I couldn't!' said Karen. 'I haven't been invited.'

'Yes, you have ... I've invited you!' Karen really would have to learn to be a bit more pushy. It didn't do to be too nice in the world of ballet. 'Look, you've got to come,' said Jessamy. 'I need someone to be there, to tell me how it goes. I've never done it on stage before – it might be disastrous.'

'It won't be,' said Karen.

'Well, but I still need someone there who knows about ballet. Everyone else just goes ooh and ah and says why don't I dance on my toes. They don't know the first thing about it. I need a proper dancer's opinion.'

Karen, though plainly flattered, said, 'Couldn't you ask your mum?'

'Mum's busy teaching.' And anyway, Belinda Tarrant always kept well out of anything to do with ordinary school. She never came to parents' days or open days, or even end-of-term shows. She just didn't regard it as important enough.

'You're the only person I know,' said Jessamy. 'The only one I can rely on.'

Susan and Sheela were both at the rehearsal – they were part of the chorus of frogs. They sat out front with Karen while Jessamy did her Rain Forest dance and afterwards took it upon themselves to criticise. They never had any qualms about voicing their opinions on subjects about which they were totally ignorant.

'We thought it was very good,' said Susan.

'Except for just one small thing,' said Sheela.

'What we can't understand – '

'When you've been doing ballet for so long – '

'Is why you can't go up on your toes yet.'

'We feel,' said Sheela, 'that it would be better if you went up on your toes.'

'Yes, because otherwise you're going to be dwarfed by all those hulking great tenth years standing around being tree people.'

'It can't be that difficult,' said Sheela, 'surely? I mean, even I can do it. Look!'

She demonstrated, wobbling on to her points (securely cushioned in their expensive Nike trainers) and grabbing hold of Susan to maintain her balance.

'I mean, I expect you'd have to practise a bit, but –'

'If Sheela can do it –'

Karen caught Jessamy's eye and giggled.

'If you go on point before you're ready for it,' said Jessamy, rather coldly, 'you can ruin your feet.'

'Well, my goodness,' said Susan, 'how long does it take to be ready for it?'

'Years,' said Karen. 'Everything in ballet takes years.'

'Well, it just seems a pity, that's all . . . if no one is going to *see* her. Because the dance itself,' said Susan, 'is very nice.'

'Very effective,' said Sheela.

'And will be even better, of course, when she has the costume.'

'Ah, yes, well,' said Sheela. 'The *costume*.'

Fortunately at this point, before Karen could choke herself or Jessamy choke someone else, Mrs Richmond came up and told Susan and Sheela to hurry along or they would miss their entrance as frogs. As they scuttled away, she turned to Jessamy.

'Well, Jessamy! What can I say? That was marvellous! Exactly the sort of thing I wanted. Quite the budding choreographer, aren't you? I thought it was most ingenious. Well done!'

'Was it really all right?' said Jessamy, when she was alone with Karen.

'It was terrific,' said Karen.

'But what about that first *arabesque*? Didn't I wobble?'

116

'Only a bit, but you don't usually. I expect it was just stage fright.'

'And d'you think I'll really be dwarfed by the trees?'

'Of course you won't! That's just Susan and Sheela being silly.'

'Whatever you do – ' Mrs Richmond had come back. She tapped Jessamy on the shoulder as she passed ' – for goodness' sake don't go breaking any bones or twisting any ankles before we get to the end of term! We're relying on you ... you're our star turn!'

That night in bed, Jessamy had yet another of her bright ideas. (To be fair, really, it had been Mrs Richmond's bright idea – not that Mrs Richmond was aware of it.)

It came to Jessamy just as she was falling asleep. It niggled at her for the rest of the night and stayed with her all day Sunday.

'It is the *best* idea,' thought Jessamy, 'that I have ever had.'

It might have been the best idea, but sometimes even the best ideas have a big BUT attached to them. In this case it was a particularly big but. Jessamy wrestled with it right through Sunday night and into Monday morning. She was still wrestling as she walked into the gym, to find Karen, as usual, already hard at work. Karen paused in her *pliés* and turned a tragic face towards her.

'They've started,' she said.

'Started what?' said Jessamy, still wrestling.

'Pulling it down.'

'Pulling what down?'

'The house! I passed it on the bus. They're taking the roof off!'

Bother, thought Jessamy. They would have to go and start this morning, wouldn't they? This was emotional blackmail. Now she wouldn't have any choice.

'I was hoping they'd leave it till after Christmas. Now I won't be able to go there any more!'

'Yes. Well. Never mind that.' Jessamy drew herself up in regal fashion, like Belinda Tarrant. 'We have work to do.'

Karen's lower lip trembled: she had obviously been looking for sympathy. Well, she wasn't going to get it. There were more important things at stake.

'I have decided,' said Jessamy, 'that instead of just doing exercises all the time you ought to learn my Rain Forest dance.'

'B –'

'For one thing – ' Jessamy held up a hand, imperiously silencing whatever objections Karen might be going to voice ' – it will be something different. For another thing it will extend you. And for another thing, I'm the teacher and you promised to do what I say. And I say,' said Jessamy, 'that we shall do a twenty-minute *barre* and then we shall start on the Rain Forest.'

Karen had watched Jessamy so many times that she almost knew the Rain Forest dance by heart. (Jessamy secretly thought that she had probably practised it in the studio at the Noran School. It was what Jessamy herself would have done.)

'I'll never be as good as you at *pirouettes*,' sighed Karen.

'No, but your *arabesques* are far better. You didn't wobble once. We'll work on it again tomorrow,' said Jessamy, as she took off her shoes and put them in the special red shoe bag that Jack had made for her (Jack having time on her hands now that she was a lady of leisure).

'What sort of costume are you going to wear?' Karen wanted to know.

The costume was going to be almost exactly as Jessamy had envisaged it – a headdress of brightly coloured feathers and all the rest a deep dark emerald green. Green shoes, green leotard, with sleeves and a high neck – even her face and hands were going to be covered in green make-up.

'It sounds wonderful,' sighed Karen. 'Will they send the local papers to take photographs?'

For a moment, Jessamy felt a slight pang. She reminded herself firmly that she was *making a sacrifice*. And what, after all, was a local paper?

'I expect they'll send someone,' she said, carelessly. 'They usually do.'

And then they had these really yucky captions – YOUNG BALLET STAR, LITTLE BALLERINA – which made Jessamy cringe and enraged everyone at the Academy. Really, not being in the local paper was only a very small part of the sacrifice.

'Will your mum and dad come and watch?' said Karen, wistfully.

'Dad might not, but I'm going to make sure that Mum does!'

Mum coming was the whole point of the exercise: Mum had to have the evidence of her own eyes.

Jessamy cornered Belinda Tarrant that same evening, when she arrived back from teaching.

'Mum – '

'What do you want, Jessamy? Can't it wait till morning?'

'I never see you in the mornings!'

'Whose fault is that? If you will get up at some unearthly hour – '

'I have to. Mum! Listen.'

Belinda Tarrant groaned. 'Must I? All I want is my hot bath and my dry Martini!'

'It won't take a minute. I want you to come to the end-of-term show.'

'What, at Coombe Hurst?' Belinda Tarrant rattled ice cubes into her Martini glass. She sounded surprised, and rather put out. 'What do you want me to come to that for? I thought you said it was tacky.'

'Jack said that, not me.'

'So isn't it tacky?'

'Well – yes; I suppose it is, quite.' Coombe Hurst didn't have a reputation for drama. The only reason the papers came was because of LOCAL BALLERINA'S DAUGHTER DANCES IN SCHOOL SHOW.

'In that case – ' slosh, gurgle went the Martini into the Martini glass ' – why do you want me to come? I never have before.'

'Yes, well – that's why,' said Jessamy. 'If you and Dad – '

'Oh, it's no use trying to rope your dad in! He's off to Winnipeg. He won't be back till Christmas Eve.'

'All right, you, then. I want *you* to come. I want you

to see my Rain Forest dance. It's – it's very important,'
said Jessamy.

'Why? Is it a choreographic masterpiece?'

'No, but I want to know what you think of it.'

'You could dance it for me in the studio.'

'*No*! It's not the same. I want you to *be* there. It's
only short,' said Jessamy. You could be home again by
nine o'clock.'

'Oh, very well! Anything for peace and quiet. Get
me a ticket and remind me nearer the date. I'll do my
best. I can't say fairer than that.'

Was it really so much to ask? wondered Jessamy.
There were moments – not very often, just now and
again – when she was almost tempted to wish that
she had ordinary parents. *Normal* parents. Parents who
automatically came to the end-of-term show. Parents
who didn't keep flying off to Winnipeg and Frankfurt
and New York. Parents who behaved like parents.

She grumbled about it to Karen, next day in the gym.

'They're not normal, my parents aren't.'

'Well, of *course* they aren't.' Karen said it reverently.
'They're famous dancers.'

'I don't see why that has to make them abnormal.'

Karen thought about it.

'I suppose perhaps famous people aren't ever the
same as ordinary people.'

'No, they're a *pain*.'

'I bet you wouldn't like it if they were ordinary.'

'No, and I bet you wouldn't like it,' retorted Jessamy,
'if you had to live with them!'

'I would.' Karen's face had gone all rapt and dreamy,

the way it often did when Jessamy talked about her family. 'I'd give anything to have parents like yours.'

Jessamy snorted.

'Is your gran going to turn up for the end-of-term show?'

'Yes! She wants to see you dance. She's really looking forward to it.'

'There! You see? That's what I call a *normal* parent. Not like mine, having to be bullied into it. And she's only your gran. I bet you wouldn't swop her . . . if you could have my mum and dad and go to ballet school, and I could have your gran and not go to ballet school . . . I bet you wouldn't, would you?'

'I – ' Karen opened her mouth and closed it again. Her cheeks grew pink. Jessamy could see the struggle going on inside her.

'*Would* you?' said Jessamy.

'I suppose I wouldn't if it meant not having Gran.'

'So there you are, then!'

Karen hung her head.

'I'm not tough enough,' she said, 'am I?'

'Doesn't matter.' Jessamy picked up her school bag and slung it over her shoulder. 'It'll all work out.'

'I don't see how it can,' said Karen.

'It can 'cause I'm telling you it can.'

'How?' Karen hurried after her. 'How can you be so sure?'

'Just wait,' said Jessamy. 'You'll see!'

9

The end-of-term show had two performances, one on Friday, one on Saturday. The reporters from the local newspapers always came on the Saturday, because everyone reckoned that the second performance was the better one. Belinda Tarrant had rolled her eyes at the thought of giving up her Saturday evening to watch 'a bunch of untalented amateurs – present company excepted, of course', but Jessamy had bought her a ticket and marked the date in her diary in enormous red letters that couldn't possibly be missed, so now she had no excuse for not turning up.

Karen's gran, originally, had been going to come on the Friday. 'She has her friends round on Saturdays,' said Karen, 'and they play whist.'

'Tell her to bring her friends as well,' had said Jessamy.

Karen had looked at her, doubtfully. Jessamy realised that it did sound rather big-headed, instructing Karen's gran to bring her friends along just so that they could watch her dance, but that couldn't be helped. It was essential she came on the Saturday. Unless, of course –

But no, that wouldn't be any good, even if Jessamy *were* prepared to sacrifice herself totally and utterly, which she wasn't sure that she was. After all, she was the one who had gone to the trouble of choreographing the dance; it wasn't fair to expect her to give up everything. She was giving up quite enough as it was. And anyway, she had bullied her mum into coming on the Saturday she couldn't change the day now.

'Honestly,' said Jessamy, 'Saturday is the *only* day. Friday will be dreadful, it always is. *Please* ask her to come on Saturday . . . *please*!'

It was the first time Jessamy had ever asked anything of Karen. She could see that it put Karen in an awkward position, but if she wouldn't be ruthless on her own behalf then someone had to be ruthless for her.

'I mean, she can play whist any Saturday,' said Jessamy, 'can't she?'

Karen, reluctantly, admitted that she could.

'So will you ask her? *Please*? Tell her it's for me.'

'All right,' said Karen.

So now not only Karen's gran but two of her gran's friends were coming, as well. Jessamy rubbed her hands, gleefully. How easy it was to talk people into doing what you wanted them to do!

The dress rehearsal was a disaster, but dress rehearsals always were. Sheela, leading the tree frog chorus, led it on in the wrong place, in the middle of someone else's scene; a great hulking brute of a sixth former crashed into a rather fragile piece of scenery and crushed it; the stage manager (another sixth former) brought the curtain down before Jessamy had done her second solo.

'Doesn't matter,' said Susan, cheerfully. 'A bad dress rehearsal means a good first night. That's what they say in the theatre, isn't it?'

'Is it?' said Jessamy, gloomily.

'Well, you ought to know!' said Susan.

Karen, who had come to watch the rehearsal, suppressed a giggle. She found Susan and Sheela a perpetual source of amusement. Jessamy said nothing. She rather suspected that at Coombe Hurst a bad dress rehearsal might quite likely mean an even worse first night, but the first night didn't really matter. It was the second night that was important.

'You will be here nice and early,' she said to Karen, 'won't you?'

'Gran always gets everywhere early,' said Karen. 'She's terrified of being late.'

'Good! Do you want to try my costume on?'

'Yes, *please*!' said Karen.

The costume fitted Karen perfectly. Apart from having slightly longer legs than Jessamy, her measurements were almost exactly the same. Even the green-dyed ballet shoes, being soft, were the right size. (Just as well they weren't using point shoes. That would have been more difficult.)

'Goodness!' said Mrs Richmond, coming into the dressing room. 'I thought for a moment you were Jessamy!'

'She looks really good,' said Jessamy, 'doesn't she?'

'She does,' said Mrs Richmond. (How was it Mrs Richmond could see it and not Jessamy's lousy rotten family?) 'Are you another dancer, Karen? I didn't realise that. Why didn't we have a *pas de deux*? It would have been rather nice.'

'Next year,' said Jessamy, 'we will.'

Apart from a piece of scenery collapsing and one of the tree frogs tripping over its own feet, the first night wasn't as bad as Jessamy had feared. Her Rain Forest dance went well – her *arabesque* didn't wobble, her *pirouettes* were spot on – and everyone came gushing up afterwards, the way they always did.

'So this is Belinda Tarrant's little girl?'

'Chip off the old block, eh?'

'Following in mother's footsteps – '

'They say it runs in families.'

All the things that Jessamy had heard a million times before. Once she had lapped it up and been in danger of growing big-headed, but now she was used to it, and was old enough, in any case, to know that people will always come flocking round the child of famous parents. Of course she enjoyed being the centre of attention; that was only natural. And of course any artist was always anxious to be reassured at the end of a performance: Jessamy was no exception. But for all that, there wasn't a single person whose opinion she really valued; not as she valued Mum and Dad's.

It would have been nice, reflected Jessamy, rather wistfully, as she removed her green make-up, if just for once her mum *had* come to see her. For a moment she almost wavered – but then she thought of Karen's gran giving up her Saturday evening whist, and Karen's gran's friends giving up *their* Saturday evening whist, and why should they be expected to do that just to watch the great Belinda Tarrant's spoilt brat?

It's true, thought Jessamy, confronting her image in the mirror: I have been spoilt. Dancing lessons practically the moment she could walk, kissed by Rudolph Nureyev (not that she could remember it), best seats at the theatre, Gelsey Kirkland's ballet shoe (just one of many), signed photographs, autograph book filled to the brim with famous signatures, all the great ballets and many of the greatest dancers there for her to see on video, just whenever she wanted. When you looked at it like that, you wondered how other people – ordinary people – ever stood a chance.

Firmly, Jessamy replaced the lid on her tin of cold cream (full stage make-up box, given to her by the grateful director of one of the ballet companies her dad had worked for. Dad was always bringing her back these little presents from his trips abroad). If she had really been so desperate to have Belinda Tarrant come and watch her she could have talked her into it last year. Last year it hadn't occurred to her – and if she was to be honest it wouldn't have occurred to her this year either, if it hadn't been for Karen. Mum saw Jessamy dance almost every day of the week; it was someone else's turn, now.

Jessamy set off early in the car with Elke for the Saturday evening performance. Belinda Tarrant was talking on the telephone to America. She had been talking for the last half hour. Jessamy mouthed urgently to her, 'You will come, won't you?'

'She will come,' said Elke. 'I remind her.'

'You promise?' said Jessamy.

Elke nodded, gravely. 'I promise.'

There was one good thing about Elke: you could rely on her.

Jessamy was dropped at the school gates. It was too early yet for any of the audience to be arriving, and even too early for most of the performers. She made her way into school and along the empty corridors until she came to the music rooms, which had been turned into dressing rooms for the occasion. Cautiously, she opened the door of Room C – Tree Frogs, Humming Birds and Jessamy. Good! No one there.

Jessamy sat down and waited.

A humming bird from Year 8 was the first to arrive. She looked at Jessamy tenderly cradling one bare foot, and obviously decided that this was just something which ballet dancers did. Jessamy said nothing, but ostentatiously massaged her ankle.

A group of tree frogs then turned up, including Susan and Sheela. No one took the least scrap of notice of Jessamy massaging her ankle. Dancers were always prodding and poking at bits of themselves, especially their feet. Susan and Sheela were having an argument about whose fault it was that last night half the tree frogs had ended up with their backs facing the audience.

'I told you, it's because they *turned* the wrong way.'

'Yes, but *why* did they turn the wrong way? You're the one that's supposed to be leading us!'

'I did lead you. It's not my fault if people don't watch what I'm doing and can't tell left from right.'

Jessamy stood up, on one leg, carefully lowered her other to the ground and let out a loud yelp. The argument stopped. Everyone turned to look at her.

'Now what's the matter?' said Sheela.

'What have you done?' said Susan.

Jessamy sank back, groaning, on to her seat.

'I think I've ricked my ankle.'

128

'Ohmygod!' said Sheela. 'That's fatal, isn't it? For a dancer?'

'Shall I get Mrs Richmond?' said Susan. 'I'll see if I can find her!'

Susan galloped off. Sheela, morbidly hopeful, said, 'Have you broken it?'

'Twisted it,' said Jessamy, 'I think.'

'How?' said a humming bird.

'Coming down the stairs ... I tripped over something.'

'If it's ruined your career,' said Sheela, who had plans for becoming a solicitor, 'you could probably sue.'

'It won't – ruin my career,' said Jessamy, heroically wincing as she probed at herself, 'but I don't think I'm – going to be able to – dance – tonight.'

If she had expected a horrified hush to fall upon the room, she was disappointed. (*Amateurs*. They were all *amateurs*.)

'Not to worry,' said a humming bird, comfortingly. 'It's not that important. After all, you're only a sort of extra.'

Jessamy gave her a look of cold contempt. She might only be a sort of extra – though embellishment was the word she personally would have chosen – but without the Rain Forest dance the show had no pretensions to quality at all. Just a gaggle of tree frogs who couldn't tell which way they were supposed to be going, a few moth-eaten monkeys, some humming birds that squawked about the stage like chickens, and half the sixth form hanging about with creepers while the other half solemnly intoned ecological messages in blank verse.

129

They needed Jessamy's Rain Forest dance to wake the audience up.

'Fortunately,' continued the idiotic humming bird, 'it's the play that people have come to see.'

'Yes, you mustn't worry,' said Sheela, in soothing tones. 'It's not as if anything depends on you.'

Jessamy began to feel rather alarmed (as well as indignant). They were sabotaging her plans! At this rate they would simply do away with her dances altogether.

Mrs Richmond came hurrying in, with Susan and the school nurse. (What was she doing here? Come to watch the performance, presumably. Jessamy hadn't been expecting that.)

'Jessamy!' said Mrs Richmond. 'What's all this I hear?'

Jessamy pulled a suffering face.

'I tripped coming down the stairs... I think I've twisted my ankle.'

'Let Nurse have a look at it.'

'There's nothing to see, but it hurts when I stand on it,' said Jessamy.

'Does it hurt when I do this?'

'Ow! Yes.'

'How about this?'

'Mmm... a little bit.'

'Well, I don't think you've actually sprained it, but I'll put a bandage on for you and you'd better not risk dancing.'

'I would risk it,' said Jessamy, 'but I just can't stand on it.'

'Oh, dear!' said Mrs Richmond. 'What a thing to

happen! I do feel guilty . . . I shouldn't have gone putting ideas into your head.'

'It was an accident,' said Jessamy.

'I'm sure it was! I'm sure you didn't do it on purpose. Never mind, it can't be helped. We'll just have to – '

'Karen could take over.' Jessamy leaped in quickly, before Mrs Richmond, like the rest of them, could decide that the dance was dispensable. 'She knows it by heart – we've practised it together.'

'Really? Where is Karen? Is she coming tonight?'

'Yes, with her gran. I should think they're probably already here. She said her gran always gets to places early.'

'And you really think she could do it?'

She'd better be able to do it, thought Jessamy, after all the trouble I've been to.

'I know she could,' said Jessamy. 'She's a really good dancer.'

'Well – ' Mrs Richmond hesitated. 'We could just cut it out, though it seems a shame, when it frames the work so well. And it would seem a pity to waste your lovely choreography. I'll go and see if Karen's out there. I'll see how she feels.'

This, thought Jessamy, was the real test. If Karen let her down – but surely she wouldn't?

'Oh, you poor *thing*!' said Susan. 'This is what dancers hate most, isn't it? Other people getting to dance their roles.'

'Doesn't really bother me,' said Jessamy, bravely. 'I danced the first night.'

'But the press is here,' said Susan. 'They'll get pictures of her and not of you. That's not fair!'

'I don't mind,' said Jessamy. 'I've had my picture in the paper loads of times.'

A few minutes later, Mrs Richmond arrived back in the dressing room accompanied by an apprehensive but excited Karen.

'Jessamy! What have you done?'

Jessamy pulled a face.

'The same as you did. It's nothing very bad, but it hurts to walk on. It's just as well I made you learn those steps.'

'Do you really think you'll be all right, Karen?' Mrs Richmond still sounded doubtful.

Karen exchanged glances with Jessamy. Jessamy nodded, vigorously.

'I'll try,' said Karen.

Nurse Rendall insisted that Jessamy stay in the dressing room, with her leg propped on a chair, until just before the curtain was due up.

'We'll smuggle you in at the last minute; you can sit at the back with me. Or have you got someone coming? Would you rather sit with them?'

'No, I'll sit at the back,' said Jessamy.

If she sat at the front with her mum, Belinda Tarrant would quite likely decide to leave there and then. 'I didn't come here to waste my time watching some pudding-faced nobody!'

If Jessamy sat at the back, she wouldn't discover until the curtain went up and by then it would be too late. Jessamy didn't think that even her mum would be rude enough to walk out once the curtain had gone up.

'I'm scared,' whispered Karen, as Jessamy helped her

on with her costume. 'I can't remember any of the steps!'

'You will,' promised Jessamy. 'As soon as you're on stage you will. It's something that happens.'

'Has it ever happened to you?'

'Lots of times,' lied Jessamy. It never had, but she had read enough books to know that it happened to other people. 'All you've got to do is just remember the *first* step – ' She sketched it out, as best she could, with her bandaged foot. 'Once you've done that, the rest will come.'

'I hope s–so,' said Karen, through chattering teeth.

Jessamy hoped so, too. Karen didn't realise how much was depending on her performance. Suppose she made a complete mess of it? It didn't bear thinking about!

So I won't think about it, thought Jessamy, hobbling into the hall on the arm of Nurse Rendall seconds before the show was due to start. What was the point of torturing yourself when the worst might never happen?

The lights were already dimming as Jessamy and Nurse Rendall took their places, so she didn't have a chance to pick out Belinda Tarrant in the front row, though she thought she caught a glimpse of her red hair. Good old Elke! You could always count on her.

The curtain went up with a satisfying swoosh (at the dress rehearsal it had become stuck half way) and there, in a pool of green light, arms symmetrically framed above her head, stood the Spirit of the Rain Forest. Jessamy took a deep breath.

Slowly, Karen lowered her arms. *And –*

Echappé – relevé – relevé devant –

Jessamy let out her breath. She would be all right, now. It was the first steps which mattered.

Karen's Spirit of the Rain Forest was different from Jessamy's. It was more mystical, for a start. Jessamy, when she was dancing it, always felt that she was fighting a battle – a battle for the rain forest. With Karen you felt that she *was* the rain forest. Harm the forest and you harmed her. Her *pirouettes* might not be as diamond hard and precise, but her *arabesque* was a perfect line from fingertip to toe.

Jessamy, sitting next to Nurse Rendall, had the double satisfaction of seeing her own work performed by her own pupil. She felt almost as proud as if she had performed it herself. Not even Belinda Tarrant could fail to be impressed!

As soon as the curtain came down for the last time (and a bashful Karen had taken her curtain call), Jessamy sprang up from her seat.

'Watch your ankle!' cried Nurse Rendall.

'It's a bit better now,' said Jessamy. 'Sitting down seems to have cured it.'

'Well, don't go rushing about. You can't afford to take any chances.'

Jessamy forced herself to walk slowly and carefully down the rows of seats. Mum was right at the front, in the centre (special treatment because of being Belinda Tarrant).

'Mum, d– '

Jessamy stopped. Where had she gone? Surely she hadn't *left*?

'Excuse me, was there someone sitting in this seat?' she said to the lady who had the seat on the other side.

The lady shook her head. (She was wearing a red furry hat that looked like hair.)

'No,' she said, 'there wasn't.'

Jessamy swallowed.

'Not even . . . at the beginning?'

'No, not all evening.'

Jessamy's cheeks turned crimson. Mum hadn't come! She had let her down! After she had *promised* –

'Jess?'

A familiar voice made her spin round. Saul was forging his way towards her.

'Why weren't you dancing?'

'I twisted my ankle. Where's Mum? Why isn't she here? Why are you here?'

'Second-best. I got home and found Elke in a flap. It seems our twitty-minded sister decided to start having her baby and your twitty-minded mother couldn't resist the opportunity to go dashing off to participate.'

'*Mum*? You mean she'd rather go and watch a baby being born than – ' Jessamy's eyes filled with self-pitying tears. After all the sacrifices she had made! 'How *could* she?'

'My sentiments precisely,' said Saul. 'There's a baby being born every second.'

'She doesn't even like them!'

'So she says. Beneath the flinty exterior there obviously beats a heart of pure marshmallow. So, anyway, I came instead, albeit twenty minutes late, expecting to see my littler and less twitty-minded sister performing miracles of her own devising, and what do I see instead? Some other child performing the miracles on her behalf . . . who is she, by the way?'

Jessamy blew rather fiercely at her nose.

'Karen.'

'Who's K – oh! I remember. Wasn't she the one who came with you that day? The little blonde?'

Jessamy sniffed.

'Who's her teacher?'

'Hasn't got one.'

'Well, who used to be?'

'No one used to be. She's never had one.'

'What do you mean, she's never had one? Who taught her to do all that?'

'She did, mostly.'

'By herself?'

'*Yes.* By herself. What everyone says is impossible.'

'I'd have said it was.'

'Well, it's not,' said Jessamy, ''cause she's done it. All I did was help her with her *pirouettes.*'

'Yes, they are her weakest point. She needs to do some work on those. But other than that – ' Saul shook his head. 'I don't believe it! She's having you on.'

'She is not,' hissed Jessamy. 'She's never had a proper lesson in her life, she j – '

'All right, all right!' Saul backed away, hands held up in protest. 'You don't have to get shirty!'

'Well, but – ' Jessamy's eyes filled again with angry tears. First Mum letting her down, now Saul not believing her!

'Hey, hey! What's all this?' Saul tilted her chin with a finger. 'Just because Mum didn't turn up?'

'She promised that she would!'

'Yeah, I know. Elke said – She seemed to think it was important. But does it really matter,' said Saul, 'since you weren't able to dance anyway?'

'I didn't want her to see me dance! I didn't care about her seeing me dance!'

'Ah! You wanted her to see the choreography? Well, I've seen it. I'll tell her. I th– '

'I didn't want her to see the choreography! I wanted her to see Karen!'

'To see *Karen*? But – ' Saul stopped. 'Hang about! Just what exactly happened to that ankle of yours?'

'Nothing, if you must know!'

'I see.' Saul nodded, slowly. 'The penny begins to drop . . . all part of a grand plan, eh? Foiled at the eleventh hour by our twitty-minded sister . . . well, look, cheer up! All is not lost. *I* came – I saw. I can report.'

'You mean about – about Karen?'

'Sure. Why not? Any kid that can get that far on her own deserves a break. Leave it to me. I'll have a word with her.'

Jessamy said breathlessly, 'With Mum? Or with Karen?'

'I meant with Mum, but if you think Karen would like me to have a word with her, too – '

'She'd be delirious!' said Jessamy.

'Very well. Lead me to her. Let's go and make her delirious.'

Karen blushed so fiercely fiery red when Jessamy appeared backstage with Saul that Jessamy almost expected her to burst into flames.

Saul said, 'That was very good, young lady. I congratulate you! But we must do something about those *pirouettes.*'

Karen blushed even deeper.

'They're better than they were,' said Jessamy. As an afterthought she added, 'She couldn't do them at all before.'

'Before what?'

'Before I taught her,' said Jessamy.

Saul pressed a finger to Jessamy's nose.

'You,' he said, 'stick to dancing. And to choreography. That wasn't half bad. Leave teaching to those as knows how.'

'But th –'

'Enough,' said Saul. 'Have faith. I will do what I can.'

Jessamy paused only long enough to whisper in Karen's ear – 'He was really impressed! He couldn't believe you'd never had any lessons. He's going to talk to Mum!' – before springing joyously up the stairs after Saul. She just managed to put in a little hobble at the last minute.

'Now, look here,' said Saul.

It was Sunday evening, in the kitchen. Belinda Tarrant had arrived home full of baby talk. Jacquetta had had a little boy. He weighed nine pounds two ounces and looked just like Saul had when he was born. He was obviously going to be a dancer.

'He has a dancer's feet!'

Saul looked at Jessamy across the kitchen table and shook his head. Elke, serious as ever, said, 'How can one tell? When so young?'

'One can't,' said Saul, 'is the answer to that.'

138

'I can,' said Belinda Tarrant. 'That child is a dancer if ever I saw one.'

'Now, look here,' said Saul for the second time. 'Can we stop babbling about babies? Can I get a word in edgeways? I've got to get back to town in a minute. But before I do – '

'Yes, yes! Before you do? You can always tell a dancer's feet. At least, I can.'

'Before I do,' said Saul; 'talking of children born to be dancers, last night I watched an eleven-year-old who's never had a dancing lesson in her life and has more talent in her little toe than most of your Academy brats have in all their great clumsy feet put together.'

'Oh?' Belinda Tarrant sat up straight, babies abruptly forgotten. 'Where did you see her?'

'At Jess's school. Taking Jess's place because Jess had – um – how can one phrase it? Temporarily put herself out of commission. On purpose. Only you'd gone off babying so it was a bit of a wasted effort, except that fortunately I was there, and I'm telling you, you ought to take a look at this child because in my opinion she could well be star material.'

'Really?' Belinda Tarrant turned, accusingly, to Jessamy. 'Why haven't you ever mentioned her?'

'Oh, *Mum*!' wailed Jessamy.

'What, you have mentioned her?'

'Over and over!'

'I gather,' said Saul, 'that in your usual inimitable fashion you said you were not a charity institution for other people's pudding-faced offspring. Or words to that effect.'

'Yes, I very likely did. Because I'm not. On the other hand, if it's a question of real talent – '

'It is,' said Saul. 'You can take my word for it.'

'I see. Well, in that case – ' Belinda Tarrant turned back to Jessamy. 'I take it you have her telephone number? You'd better give her a ring and arrange for her to come round to the studio some time.'

Jessamy hesitated.

'She can't afford to pay anything,' she said. 'She lives with her gran and her gran's really poor and her grandad killed himself so she could have an education only her gran thinks he meant book learning and – '

Belinda Tarrant waved a hand.

'The money is immaterial. Let me see the child dance.'

Jessamy thrust her chair back.

'I'll do it right away! When can she come?'

'Tomorrow, if you like. You might as well bring her with you after school. And Jessamy – ' Mum reached out a hand, pulling Jessamy towards her. 'I'm sorry, darling, that I let you down. It was naughty of me. I can only say that it's not every day one becomes a grandmother – but that's no excuse! It was most unprofessional. And what was worse, it upset you.'

'That's all right,' said Jessamy.

'Am I forgiven?' Mum held up her face for a kiss. Jessamy pecked, perfunctorily, at her cheek. She just wanted to rush now and tell Karen.

Belinda Tarrant laughed. 'Oh, I can see you're impatient! Go on, off you go, and break the good news.'

140

Like a bullet from a gun, Jessamy shot across the room, up the stairs to the hall, up more stairs to her bedroom. She could have used the telephone in the kitchen, but she didn't want to talk in front of the others. This was between her and Karen.

She snatched up the receiver and dialled Karen's number.

'Hallo?' said Karen.

'It's me,' said Jessamy. 'Listen! Saul's spoken to Mum and Mum says I'm to bring you with me after school tomorrow! She wants to see you dance.'

'Oh, Jessamy . . .' Karen's voice was hardly above a whisper. 'If this works out I'll be in your debt for ever and ever!'

'It will work out,' said Jessamy. 'I have good feelings about it. And you won't be in my debt – you'll be in Saul's . . . I didn't do anything.'

'You taught me how to do *pirouettes*!'

'Didn't even do that very well, according to Saul.'

There was a pause.

'So how is your ankle?' said Karen.

'My ankle?' Just in time, she remembered. 'Oh, that's all right.'

'Goodness! It got better quickly.'

'Yes, well, it wasn't very bad.'

'Like a sort of one-hour sprain, really.'

'Well – yes. I suppose it was, really.'

'Just enough to stop you dancing.'

'Oh, I couldn't have danced,' said Jessamy.

A sound suspiciously like a giggle came down the line.

'What are you laughing about?' said Jessamy.

141

'Nothing,' said Karen. 'See you tomorrow, in the gym. Do you think we ought to work on my *pirouettes*?'

'Yes,' said Jessamy. 'I think we'd better!'

Other great reads ✗ from **Red Fox**

Further Red Fox titles that you might enjoy reading are listed on the following pages. They are available in bookshops or they can be ordered directly from us.

If you would like to order books, please send this form and the money due to:

ARROW BOOKS, BOOKSERVICE BY POST, PO BOX 29, DOUGLAS, ISLE OF MAN, BRITISH ISLES. Please enclose a cheque or postal order made out to Arrow Books Ltd for the amount due, plus 75p per book for postage and packing to a maximum of £7.50, both for orders within the UK. For customers outside the UK, please allow £1.00 per book.

NAME_____

ADDRESS_____

_____

Please print clearly.

Whilst every effort is made to keep prices low, it is sometimes necessary to increase cover prices at short notice. If you are ordering books by post, to save delay it is advisable to phone to confirm the correct price. The number to ring is THE SALES DEPARTMENT 071 (if outside London) 973 9700.

Action-Packed Drama with Red Fox Fiction!

SIMPLE SIMON   Yvonne Coppard

Simon isn't stupid – he's just not very good at practical things. So when Mum collapses, it's Cara, his younger sister who calls the ambulance and keeps a cool head. Simon plans to show what he can do too, in a crisis, but his plan goes frighteningly wrong . . .
ISBN 0 09 910531 4   £2.99

LOW TIDE   William Mayne

Winner of the Guardian Children's Fiction Award.

   The low tide at Jade Bay leaves fish on dry land and a wreck high on a rock. Is this the treasure ship the divers have been looking for? Three friends vow to find out – and find themselves swept away into adventure.
ISBN 0 09 918311 0   £3.50

THE INTRUDER   John Rowe Townsend

It isn't often that you meet someone who claims to be you. But that's what happens to Arnold Haithwaite. The real Arnold has to confront the menacing intruder before he takes over his life completely.
ISBN 0 09 999260 4   £3.50

GUILTY   Ruth Thomas

Everyone in Kate's class says that the local burglaries have been done by Desmond Locke's dad, because he's just come out of prison. Kate and Desmond think otherwise and set out to prove who really is *guilty*.
ISBN 0 09 918591 1   £2.99

Other great reads from **Red Fox**

Top teenage fiction from Red Fox

PLAY NIMROD FOR HIM   Jean Ure

Christopher and Nick are each other's only friend.
Isolated from the rest of the crowd, they live in their
own world of writing and music. Enter lively, popular
Sal who tempts Christopher away from Nick . . .
ISBN 0 09 985300 0   £2.99

HAMLET, BANANAS AND ALL THAT JAZZ
Alan Durant

Bert, Jim and their mates vow to live dangerously –
just as Nietzsche said. So starts a post-GCSEs summer
of girls, parties, jazz, drink, fags . . . and tragedy.
ISBN 0 09 997540 8   £3.50

ENOUGH IS TOO MUCH ALREADY
Jan Mark

Maurice, Nina and Nazzer are all re-sitting their
O levels but prefer to spend their time musing over
hilarious previous encounters with strangers, hamsters,
wild parties and Japanese radishes . . .
ISBN 0 09 985310 8   £2.99

BAD PENNY   Allan Frewin Jones

Christmas doesn't look good for Penny this year. She's
veggy, feels overweight, *and* The Lizard, her horrible
father has just turned up. Worse still, Roy appears –
Penny's ex whom she took a year to get over.
ISBN 0 09 985280 2   £2.99

CUTTING LOOSE   Carole Lloyd

Charlie's horoscope says to get back into the swing of
things, but it's not easy: her Dad and Gran aren't
speaking, she's just found out the truth about her
mum, and is having severe confused spells about her
lovelife. It's time to cut loose from all binding ties, and
decide what she wants and who she really is.
ISBN 0 09 91381 X   £3.50

Other great reads from Red Fox

Enjoy Jean Ure's stories of school and home life.

JO IN THE MIDDLE

The first of the popular Peter High series. When Jo starts at her new school, she determines never again to be plain, ordinary Jo-in-the-middle.

ISBN 0 09 997730 3   £2.99

FAT LOLLIPOP

The second in the Peter High series. When Jo is invited to join the Laing Gang, she's thrilled – but she also feels guilty because it means she's taking Fat Lollipop's place.

ISBN 0 09 997740 0   £2.99

A BOTTLED CHERRY ANGEL

A story of everyday school life – and the secrets that lurk beneath the surface.

ISBN 0 09 951370 6   £1.99

FRANKIE'S DAD

Frankie can't believe it when her mum marries horrible Billie Small and she has to go and live with him and his weedy son, Jasper. If only her real dad would come and rescue her . . .

ISBN 0 09 959720 9   £1.99

YOU TWO

A classroom story about being best friends – and the troubles it can bring before you find the right friend.

ISBN 0 09 938310 1   £1.95